Sandbar Storm

A SUMMER COTTAGE NOVEL

REBECCA REGNIER

Viv

It wasn't over. Viv looked down at her body. She was changed. Forever. Maybe she should have had reconstruction. Maybe that would make her feel more like herself.

But it was a longer recovery. And they were just boobs.

Who cared about that at her age?

Honestly, right now, she didn't know what she cared about.

She slipped on her t-shirt and tucked it into The Power Skirt.

She'd sold The Power Skirt to thousands of women, usually with her Means Business Blazer.

She did not pair her skirt with the blazer today. Today, her soft, worn old jean jacket topped off her ensemble.

Viv ran her fingers through her hair. She'd lost hair, but not because of chemo. They said it was stress. Early on, she wound up cutting her hair into a tight pixie. It was an act of defiance, or maybe it was acceptance. She wasn't sure. But now it was growing back. Weirdly. It had no style, and she didn't care. It was just hair.

She'd lost something else. She didn't know what. Viv couldn't put her finger on it.

This was supposed to be a great visit. It was supposed to be a celebration. She finished getting dressed and just felt disconnected. The exam room was a familiar place these days, but it all seemed alien. She was someone others described as comfortable in her own skin. That was another thing Viv had lost.

Her daughter, Siena, was in the waiting room. Her lithe and sunny girl was happy. She was ready to get a cake. Siena saw this as a sort of birthday event. Viv plastered a cheerful look on her face. She turned the corners of her mouth up, but try as she might, it wasn't a smile.

Her doctor told them exactly what they'd hoped for.

"It's looking great. We think we got it all!"

Dr. Hinkley had been wonderful. Truly. She had reassured Viv every step of the way. And the doctor was happy too. Happy for her.

The phrase, *we got it all.* That was the brass ring of cancer treatment. *We got it all.*

Viv looked at Siena's face upon hearing that pronouncement. Siena did a fist bump, and she hugged Viv. It was good. Viv knew it was good.

It was the thing they had hoped to hear.

The goal of her adult life as a career woman was to have it all. *Have it all.*

You can have it all had morphed into *we think we got it all.*

The first had not proved possible. Was the second?

It was, *we think.* Not *we know.*

At the height of her career as a clothing designer, mother, and wife, Viv didn't have it all any more than any other woman. Maybe her treatment didn't get it all. *Have it all, got it all.* They both swirled around her brain. Focus was hard for her. The other result of all the treatments, she was told. It would get better.

Stage 3A breast cancer, ER, PR positive, tumor grade two.

She'd learned about all the categories, subcategories, hoops, numbers, and grades since finding that little lump. A little lump combined with the lymph node and her mother's death from the same diagnosis meant a double mastectomy and radiation.

Despite the scary diagnosis, everyone kept saying, *you got this.*

Have it all, got it all, and you got this. Add that to the list of pithy three-word phrases that haunted her lately.

Viv had been told a million times, "You got this."

Maybe she did. But it felt more like the scalpel, and the radiation "got this." She'd been passive in the process. You couldn't tell cancer to get lost. You couldn't expel it via your iron will. Viv had spent the last few months holding her breath, showing her daughter she was strong, and laughing at Bret's jokes about him not being a breast man.

She'd been acting. She hadn't shown her true self. She hadn't allowed her fears to spill onto her daughter or her ex.

Bret, her ex, he was not a breast man, not by a long shot. Bret was a man's man, as it were, and while it ruined their marriage, it never ruined their love for each other. Bret, her ex, had been there for her just like Siena had.

The only one who wasn't there was Viv. She was outside of this body. She was hovering on the margin of her vitality. Her life.

Life. She was sure it was over. She agreed with everyone's affirmations. She played the role of a positive thinker. But inside, things weren't so sunny.

She was Vivian Blackwood of Vivian Blackwood Designs. They told her to try to hold on to her creativity during her treatment. But try as she might, the ideas weren't coming. The joy she used to feel in her career, in her life, was gone.

She sat at her drawing table, and nothing came.

She walked outside with her sketch book and wound up scrawling random shapes.

Viv had been the queen of great clothes for career women. She built a business that had suited women from board rooms to courtrooms. She used to have a fire for it. Had the radiation fried her creativity and the cancer? It felt like that.

Viv hadn't said it to anyone, but in her mind, even though she was "fine," it felt like she needed to get her affairs in order. That was the bottom line.

She was the artist. Siena was the organizer. Bret was the cheerleader and number cruncher. But none of it worked without Viv's designs.

She needed to wean them from depending on her creativity. Poor choice of words, she supposed. But that was it. She had no inspiration. She barely had the strength to get out of bed. She'd been faking it every single day since her diagnosis.

Viv knew her daughter and Bret would be okay without her to lead them. But that "okay" state seemed far away for her, unattainable. How did people do this? How did they shake off the worry?

During the doctor visits, the things they said about her prognosis echoed in her mind.

"Of course, we're going to want to do a monthly check, then six weeks. And then after that, every three months, and then six, and so on as we get further down the line."

Siena had written down all the information, as usual. Viv had nodded. Four weeks, three months, six months. Why not no more checks? Why not just say you're fine? Go forth and live your life. They didn't say that because that wasn't possible.

It was autumn when this had started. Eight months ago? Was that right?

She'd spent more time in hospital gowns than in her own clothing designs this year.

She was lost in her thoughts as Siena took the wheel on the way back home.

As Siena drove, there was a lilt in her voice and a smile on her lips. Viv stared out the window. She noticed the buds on the trees. It was spring. She'd made it to spring. That was something.

When they got back to the house, Bret and his partner, Travis, were waiting with champagne. They hugged her gently. She was still sore.

But it wasn't really soreness. It was numbness. Her chest felt numb where her breasts used to be.

But deeper in, where no hug could reach, it wasn't numb. It was pulsating fear.

Chapter Two

Siena

"Honey, I promise you, this is the best place! We cannot wait to get you here."

"Aunt Goldie, I appreciate it. You can't know how much." Siena was doing everything she could to keep the business going in the wake of her mom's cancer.

This idea was her best and most risky. It had to work.

Aunt Goldie was Goldie Hayes to the world. She was Siena's biological mother. Aunt Goldie was like Santa Claus to her. Aunt Goldie was always the vacation, the surprise under the tree, the sunny day. They needed Goldie right now.

Last year, Aunt Goldie had done something shocking.

She'd moved from Hollywood back to Michigan. In the middle of a P.R. crisis, her aunt had taken control and shocked everyone with her next move.

Along with being a movie star, she was now running a lakeside hotel, of all things. Her main base of operation had moved from Beverly Hills to the Irish Hills.

Siena could hardly believe the change in Aunt Goldie. She was running the Two Lakes Grove Hotel, dating a carpenter or something, and had been eating bread, along with other carbs. Shocking!

For the last eight months, Siena had tried so hard to shoulder everything. She wanted her mom to be okay and not to have to worry about the business. But she'd failed. Vivian Blackwood Designs was on the skids. No one was buying her mom's once-red-hot fashions.

Aunt Goldie had been her sounding board. She'd been the one person Siena could be honest with about her worries and fears.

It was Aunt Goldie to the rescue. Even though her mom didn't know that. On Siena's most recent call with Aunt Goldie, three other women joined in. Women Siena had heard stories about but never met.

Libby Quinn, J.J. Tucker, and Hope Venerable. There was a picture in her mother's office of the five women sitting on a raft, floating in a lake. They were all young, early teens, her mother said, and they were sunburned. Sunburn was something Siena had never been, thanks to her mother's religious anointing of sunscreen every time Siena went outdoors.

"You'll thank me one day, see these freckles on my décolletage? They're not freckles. They're dark dots of doom, waiting to get me. I've saved you from that fate." Her mom had been joking, but she'd been right about doom, shockingly right.

Aunt Goldie offered a break from all of it, and maybe more, maybe a way out of the mess the business was currently in, thanks to Siena.

"I've set up a room for you and for your mom, the best two, for as long as it takes to get you settled," Aunt Goldie explained.

Settled, that wasn't really the right word. All of this would be unsettling to her mom. Siena was making a bold move. But she was doing it for her mother. She was doing it because the old ideas weren't working.

Thanks to Siena's idea and Aunt Goldie's push, Vivian Blackwood Designs was going to open its first retail location.

Her mother was a creative force. Siena knew that. But she needed something new. She needed a challenge to bring her back to the land of the living. Department stores were too generic, and it was hard for her mom's designs to stand out. They needed the spotlight. Shopping for a Vivian Blackwood Designs piece needs to be an experience. They'd never had a boutique. They'd never curated their own store. Siena could make this work. She could revive the business. She had to.

Siena had taken charge of her mother's medical care during her cancer. She'd also been dealing with her mother's business affairs so she could focus on getting well. This was the next step. The treatments were done. The cancer was gone. It was time to shake things up.

Her mother wasn't going to stagnate if Siena had anything to say about it. Nope.

Aunt Goldie told her the Sandbar Sisters needed Viv.

Siena thought Viv needed them, to be honest. Her mother needed a new life, fun, *something*, to shake her out of the awfulness of the last year.

Siena would save the business by opening a store in Irish Hills, and she'd give her mom the gift of reconnecting with old friends.

Siena, for her part, needed that too. Siena had felt the weight of it all lately, more than she could have imagined after that first appointment. She was only twenty-three, but she felt a decade older than any of her peers.

Enter the Sandbar Sisters. They were the tonic Siena and Viv needed. When Aunt Goldie heard Siena's worries and her struggles, she convinced Siena that this was the right plan.

"I'm getting Mom packed up by the end of the week, and we'll be there for the holiday weekend. I can't wait to see the famous Irish Hills!"

"You're going to love it and brace yourself. You've got three times the aunts once you get here," Goldie said. The other women chimed in and talked over each other. And then Siena heard one say, no, it's four times.

"Four times the aunts?" Siena asked.

"Yep, forgot about Aunt Emma. She's more the great aunt, but yeah, we're going to spoil you and your mother. Safe travels!"

"Aunt Goldie, I appreciate this. She needs it. It's all I can think of to do.

"We'll be there for her and you, I promise."

Aunt Goldie was a ray of sunshine in their lives. They needed that. Her mom needed it.

"It sounds great. Thank you, and see you soon."

Siena liked the sound of sharing some of the responsibility for her mom's happiness. For the last year, it seemed like she'd held the weight of the world. Siena had happily taken control and done everything she could to get her mother through cancer. But now, she needed to get her mother to Irish Hills. In Irish Hills, there was help, a sisterhood for her mom, and salvation for the business.

Siena hadn't shared much about it with her mother. She'd spring the details on her once they got there. What Siena had done was drastic, but they needed drastic.

Siena stood up and headed for her mother's old studio. It was looking depressing. Her mother was spending a lot of time in there, but she didn't emerge with ideas or sketches. No new designs were in the pipeline. Her mother just stared a lot.

Siena swallowed and squared her shoulders. It was time to get this show on the road and level with her mother.

Chapter Three

Viv

Viv used to look through the bay window in her studio and see inspiration. The colors in the sky could be the inspiration for a blouse, a leaf could suggest the shape of a pair of earrings, and a bird on the wing could inspire a scarf.

Now she looked outside but didn't feel inspired. The spring buds were lovely, but she felt sad. Lately, all she could do was worry that this was the last time she'd see something. Everything felt like goodbye.

Her prognosis was good. She was "all clear." But she was all clear "for now."

It was that, *for now*, that had her stuck.

She had always looked ahead; she'd always felt optimistic about the future. The last few months had robbed her of more than her health. It had robbed her of that outlook. Viv crossed her arms around her own body and squeezed. She was still a little sore but not terrible. She was doing the exercises they told her to do.

The fashion rags would not believe the current appearance of

Vivian Blackwood; she'd always been the queen of the career wardrobe. These days it was loose sweatshirts and leggings. Yeah, some power suit this was.

Siena knocked lightly on her door.

"Come in, honey."

"I'm still not used to seeing this place so empty, with no colors, so weird."

"Time for someone else to fill it."

They were putting the house on the market. Viv liked that idea. Siena was taking the lead on all of it. She'd insisted on taking care of everything so Viv could focus on getting better. This house was too much work, too showy, too *too*. It felt like a thing of her past before they even moved out.

Viv kept feeling that she, too, was a thing of the past.

"Come on then, the car is packed. Dad stopped by to say goodbye."

"Okay, we better get going then."

Viv didn't much want to go on a trip, but Siena and Bret pushed the idea that it would help her brush off the blues and help her transition to whatever came next.

What did come next?

Siena was clearly up to something. Viv realized she hadn't really looked at her daughter, hadn't assessed how she'd been handling all the things thrust upon her since Viv's diagnosis. Viv had spent the last 23 years with two priorities, Siena and her designs. She'd neglected both during her treatment.

Siena was smiling, but there was a tightness to it. The corners of her mouth seemed forced upward.

"I'm so excited to visit Aunt Goldie in Irish Hills."

"What? I thought we were going to visit her in L.A."

Every time they'd visited Goldie, it had been somewhere exotic and glamorous. Goldie's own house in California was the epitome of both. Goldie Hayes lived large and liked to share it with them.

"No, actually, we're going to see her in her new digs, not her old one. Dad and Travis are waiting to see us off. We need to get rolling."

"Michigan, really?"

Viv hadn't been back to Michigan in decades. Had she missed this detail when Siena had told her about the little trip? Viv supposed it was possible. Her focus being total crap lately. But it seemed like a big detail to have zoned out on. Still, a trip to see Goldie was always good for both of them. Even if it was Michigan this time.

"Yes. I talked to Aunt Goldie, and she really wants us to visit her new place, not her old place. Her hotel sounds amazing. We've got rooms reserved, and think about it, you've not seen these old friends of yours since, what, high school? They're all back there now. Must be something in that water."

"I guess, yes, other than Goldie, I haven't been good about staying in touch."

Goldie and Viv had stayed close. First, it was because they'd both moved to California after high school. And then they were both in the arts. Their two worlds were adjacent. Finally, there was the unbreakable bond with Siena.

The rest of the Sandbar Sisters, Hope, J.J., and Libby, they were all firmly childhood friends. Beautiful memories from Dayglo summers.

For a moment, the sun-sprinkled lake flashed in her mind. She'd never gone back. Irish Hills was a summer vacation for her parents, and once her parents were gone, that was it. They had a house on the water here in upstate. There was no need to visit Michigan anymore.

"The app says it will take us about eight hours. Your friends are waiting."

Viv stood up. Siena turned to go as though it was a done deal, as though there was no changing it. Viv reached out. This seemed scary all of a sudden. These were strangers other than Goldie. She didn't have the energy for strangers.

"Honey, I don't think I'm up to that. It was all I could do to go to L.A. I don't have the bandwidth for a reunion or whatever."

Siena inhaled, and Viv could see her summoning the patience required to convey her next thought. Viv's cancer had switched their roles. Viv recalled calmly expressing life's situations to her inquisitive little girl, and now, her daughter was the one exasperated, exhausted even.

Viv realized her battle had taken a toll on her daughter just as much as it had on her.

"Mom, you need to talk to friends. You need more than I can give you. I can't be your sounding board."

"Honey, you've been just fine. It makes no sense for me to go try to make new friends, not with the current situation."

"You're all clear. You need friends, plus these are old friends. They already love you. You also need some design inspiration; this will be it. You can go back to where you first learned to sketch!"

"Honey, I don't think this is the best idea." But Viv's resolve was as strong as her abs these days. In other words, Jell-O.

"It is a good idea. Who knows about best? If you just open up a little to some girlfriend time and adventure, you'll be able to put last year in perspective and maybe even find some happy."

"I'm happy."

"This doesn't look like happy to me." Siena picked up the sketchbook of black penciled scribbles.

Viv had put too much on Siena. She could see that now, maybe for the first time. She'd been focused on her own journey, her own fight, and she'd put everything else on her daughter. Siena needed a break. She needed Viv to lift the burden.

This trip wasn't about Viv. It was about Siena, giving Siena a break.

In that light, Viv got behind the idea. A few weeks in the Irish Hills, where Siena wasn't the sole caretaker of her mother, was a good idea.

Viv felt incredible guilt. During her treatment, she was selfish, if not outwardly, at least inside. She'd only thought of her own emotions and reactions. Viv had dragged her daughter into this health thing, her upbeat daughter. Viv didn't want to be the cause of Siena's tense smile anymore.

"Alright, you're the boss, a trip to the old lake it is." Viv put on a smile now and hoped she did a better job of making it look genuine.

"Come on, Dad and Travis are in the driveway arguing about how I packed the car. Let's go."

Viv took one last look at her studio view. She'd created a lot here. She'd raised Siena here. She and Bret had hammered out their spouse to friends transition here. She'd beaten cancer here, for now. She'd loved this house. But maybe it was time to say goodbye to this place, too, like everything else.

She could at least agree that it was time for a change of scenery. She'd do this for Siena. She'd put on a brave face, a smiley one, even if she didn't feel it.

Chapter Four

Siena

Siena had never been to the Midwest. She'd grown up in New York State, and she'd vacationed on the west coast, but she'd never been to Michigan.

Siena did the driving, and her mother did a lot of sleeping. It was an eight-hour trek that Siena would have done in one go, but she worried about her mom's stamina.

They crossed from New York to Pennsylvania, spent the night just outside of Cleveland, and then set off for the last leg.

I-90 took them all the way to Toledo, Ohio. Siena let the GPS guide her from the main highways to successively smaller state routes. Ohio-109 to Michigan-52 to US-223 to Michigan-50 to 12.

Fields and farm stands were the rule, not the exception, as they closed in on Irish Hills.

It felt like mom was somewhere else, mentally. Her mother had always been so vibrant, so present, and appreciative of the moment. But since the diagnosis, it was like she'd checked out.

Siena desperately wanted to help, wanted to make a new start with her mom. Maybe Michigan could be the change of scenery they needed.

Just when she thought her mom was zoned out, she perked up as they rolled into the quaint downtown Irish Hills, Manitou Lake Road.

There was a lovely welcome sign and a gazebo with white columns separating the main street. On one side, there was scaffolding and nothing but construction. The other side, though, was picture-perfect!

It looks plucked out of Main Street at Disney, Siena thought. But she was also kind of embarrassed to think that. She knew the reverse was true. Disney was a copy of something like this.

"Wow, this place is looking pretty cute. Those buildings were gutted in the tornado, I thought," her mom said. She'd sat up straight in her seat and had rolled down the car window for the first time in their eight-hour trek.

"They look totally restored," Siena said. She noted a cute restaurant on the corner and a hardware store across town. It looked like they had a grocer and a car dealership down the way, too. Libby Quinn had plucked this town from the jaws of a developer, Siena had read.

"Is it like you remember?"

"It is. I can't believe it."

Siena would hold off just a little longer. It was best to have Aunt Goldie in the room when she dropped the bomb. No, not dropped the bomb, started their future. It was all good. Still, Siena was nervous. She'd been at the helm of the business, and her mom had trusted her, but she'd trusted her to keep things going, not turn them in a new direction.

"Yeah, they look lovely, and look, that town square that was there when I was a kid, but not as fancy."

Siena imagined get-togethers, craft shows, and all manner of fun stuff happening here. She was excited to be a part of it. She was excited to look forward to helping her mother do the same.

She was not excited to tell her mother any of it.

"Do you have any innate sense of the direction we're going for this Two Lakes Grove Hotel?"

"Maybe if I was on a bike. I didn't have a car here back in the day."

"So, how many summers did you spend here?"

"Gosh, from 1985 to 1989. After that, the tornado made this place a less than desirable vacation spot for my parents. I was only eleven when I met the girls. A couple of them were my age, and Libby and Hope were our gang leaders. To an eleven-year-old, a thirteen-year-old is the height of worldly sophistication."

"Of course," Siena said. But in truth, she didn't have a gang of girls to hang around. She had her mother and father, her Aunt Goldie, and other grownups. She'd been given access to their world, which was amazing. But now, hearing about her mom's old friends, she felt a little sad. She didn't have a BFF.

She did have her mom, and she was determined to bring her around. There was no reason this malaise should linger. This trip and this plan would be just the thing.

"So, the GPS says turn here down this way."

"Seems right."

"Wow." Siena looked beyond the downtown buildings and toward the lake.

"Yes, wow, I sort of forgot how pretty Lake Manitou could be."

Siena drove slowly and continued to glance between cottages at the water beyond.

They traveled down a main road and to one paved with gravel. But it all skirted the lakes. They were never more than a house or two's width away from a glimpse of the water.

Finally, they drove up to the Two Lakes Grove Hotel. It was easily the biggest structure they'd encountered since leaving the main drag.

The historic building was stunning.

"This building is Aunt Goldie, no question."

"She does like glamour."

And that was right; there was a glamour to this hotel. It looked like a little cousin to the famed Grand Hotel on Mackinaw or something you'd find on the beach in Coronado, California. It gleamed.

Aunt Goldie could afford the best, and it looked like she'd restored the place to her movie-star standards.

"Yeah, Aunt Goldie looks like she's doing just fine as a part-time superstar," Viv said. Siena knew her aunt had scaled back her shooting schedule, but this place revealed that she hadn't scaled back her life, not one bit.

Siena parked and came around to help her mom. She was still weak, still unsure on her feet. "Here, be careful. The gravel is tricky."

"I'm not one hundred years old."

"I know, I know. Let's leave the bags. I'll bring them in after we know where we're bunking."

"Bunking? That doesn't quite fit with the place, does it?"

"No, I mean, do they have bunks in the Chateau Marmot?" That was it. There was a cool vibe that was unexpected as they walked up the cobblestone to the grand front door.

"Do we knock?" Siena said.

Before her mother could answer, the doors flung open, and there she was, Goldie Hayes.

She glowed. She glowed in a way that shocked Siena. Her biological mother was usually pale, verged on painfully thin, and always turned out from false eyelashes to pedicured toes. This Goldie was actually a little golden from the sun. Her cheeks were plush, her figure fuller, and no question healthier.

Siena was thrilled to see this change and, again, felt vindicated about her choice. If Goldie's vibrant health was contagious, maybe Viv could catch it.

"Siena, did you get taller? How in the world?" Goldie actually brought her in for a hug. She had never been a hugger until now. Wow.

Siena hugged back hard.

"Now you," Goldie turned to Viv, and instead of the bear hug, she moved delicately to kiss Viv on the cheek and lightly embrace her. Goldie and Siena had talked a bit. Goldie knew that Viv was still raw. That was the word. After months of treatment and appointments, and doctor conversations, her mom was raw. The creative energy and spark that had been in Vivian Blackwood's eyes were gone. Instead, there was something haunted.

"You look spectacular. This place looks spectacular. I mean, this was a camp or something, right, when we used to come here?"

"Thank you, love. Yes, it's had several different incarnations. These days it's a resort hotel! We've got twelve rooms, each one themed, and, of course, my base of operations."

"I cannot believe you're not full time in L.A.," Viv said.

"I leave in the winter. You can be sure about that. It's cold as a witch's—"

"Goldie, you bellowed?" A buff-looking dude in his forties, sporting just the right amount of tight t-shirt with the logo *Cassidy Contracting* stretched across his pecs, appeared behind Aunt Goldie in the lobby. He leaned over to Goldie and kissed her on the cheek.

"Well, yes, you told me Jaden went into town to help Hope get the lunch. I needed some help with my two new guests."

"Okay, Siena and Viv, right?" the man said, pegging them correctly. He had a smile that would be at home in Hollywood and forearms equal to the task of carrying their luggage and then some. It also seemed that he did not take any crap from Aunt Goldie. He shook their hands.

"I'm Joe. Is that your Volvo? Pop the locks. I'll get after it."

"Thank you, yes, Viv is in Vineyard, and Siena is in Crystal," Goldie told him. She turned to Viv and Siena and explained, "Each of our rooms is themed to the different lakes."

"I'll come with you to help get it all sorted from the get-go," Siena said to Joe.

"Great," Goldie said, "your mother and I can catch up."

Siena left Viv to Goldie. For the first time, she felt a little lighter. Goldie would put a smile on her mother's face. She'd know how to help.

Siena followed Joe out to the car.

This was all going to work out. Siena took a deep breath, and the lake air, with a hint of lilac blossoms, seemed to confirm it.

Chapter Five

Viv

"You're too thin," Goldie said.

"You're just right." Viv loved the warmth and new softness of Goldie that she'd never seen before. Goldie had gripped tight to youth. But letting loose a bit had made her more beautiful in Viv's eyes.

Viv was happy for Goldie. Goldie was a shark, always moving, always working on the next rung of her career. She'd gotten to the top not by accident but by grit. There were thousands of beautiful blondes in Hollywood. Only a handful that made it. Goldie was one.

Viv knew that Goldie Hayes only ever let her guard down with Siena and she herself. She played with Siena, she sipped wine with Viv, she even nibbled on a carb now and again when they hung out.

Viv and Siena had always provided Goldie a break from the pressure of show business. But it was always brief, and it was always back to the discipline that kept her looking thirty at almost fifty. But now, here in Irish Hills, Goldie radiated security, confidence, comfort, and maturity. Maturity was beautiful, but not in Hollywood!

"I know, right? Who knew a little body fat could help soften the face. I'm about to take on the role of the mom of adults in this new project I'm doing for Amazon Prime. It's called *The Hour of Her Death*, about a podcaster. I'm not the lead, the podcaster. I'm her *mother*, but I am the producer. Read the book, bought the rights, and I call the shots. It's been a revelation. I'm not even getting Botox before we shoot. Ha!"

"You're a latter-day Reese Witherspoon!"

"Yeah, I wish I would have figured that out sooner. Calling my shots instead of being a slave to shots?" Goldie pointed to her forehead, which was slightly less paralyzed than the last time Viv had seen it. "Yeah. I'm loving it."

"I think you're loving the lake air and the lake hunk."

"For sure."

Just then, a fluffy little white dog, that looked more cotton ball than canine, trotted over to inspect the situation.

"Myrna! The lake agrees with you, too!"

Goldie's Bichon had a countrified bandana around her neck. The little diva used to sport a crystal doggie collar.

"Oh, she thinks she's a Golden Retriever these days. She barking at ducks like she's the sheriff of all ducks. Go on now, Myrna. I saw a squirrel outside." Myrna trotted off to patrol the grounds, apparently.

"Now get in here, sit down. The girls are on the way. But I want to catch up before they get here."

"All the girls?"

"Yes, the Sandbar Sisters in total, now that you're here."

Viv and Goldie walked arm and arm through the little lobby check-in area and toward the back of the hotel. Viv gasped. Her eyes feasted on the wall of windows; little wave caps on the blue lake twinkled like daylight stars in the panoramic view.

For a second, she just stared at the water. She flashed back to her young self. The one who charged ahead. The one who didn't worry about the future. The one who didn't drape doom around every threshold.

That was who her old friends expected. This was no longer her. Viv worried about that, about disappointing all of them.

She was tired. She wasn't ready to be "on" for anyone.

Goldie guided her to a comfortable chair. She kneeled down in front of Viv.

"I'm going to tell you something. I can see you're nervous or reticent. I get it. I did not think Irish Hills was the answer to my P.R. crisis last summer. It turned out it was the answer to a lot more than that. You just be you. The rest will work itself out."

"If someone tries to get me to go tubing, well, that's it. I'm out."

"Deal."

Viv felt some of the tension go out of her shoulders and neck. She was putting too much pressure on herself. It would be nice to see old friends. Maybe for the last time, before she — She tried to stop her mind from doing it, but it did it.

Her mind finished the thought. Maybe this was the last time she would see her old friends before she got too sick. That's what her head did, no matter how many times the doctors and the cancer support group said she should think positively. The dark thoughts finished her sentence. Behind every "you got this" and "you can do anything you set your mind to," sat, "this is the last time."

Viv put a smile on her face for Siena, for Goldie, even if inside, the last thing she felt was "go, girl."

* * *

Viv, 1989

. . .

"No way. No WAY!" Goldie squealed and applauded. She lived for applause but also gave them freely.

Libby, Hope, J.J., Goldie, and Viv watched as Keith Brady swung out on the little disk secured to the rope. The rope arced over the water. Then he let loose and did a flip into the lake.

The water splashed up, and then there was no sign of Keith.

"Great, he died. We're not supposed to be over here, and now we're in for it," J.J. said and looked around like the police were going to come and arrest them.

"We're here because Mr. Ewald is at the council meeting. They all are. Quit worrying." Libby said to J.J.

They knew all the good places. If Viv didn't have these friends, she'd spend her summers by herself reading the latest Sidney Sheldon or Danielle Steel. She'd spent more time at the Irish Hills Library than she did by the lake until she met J.J.

J.J. had spotted Viv at the store that first summer and recruited her into this girl gang. She'd showed up at Viv's family's summer rental one day and asked Viv's mom if there were any girls in this house to play with!

Viv's mom had shoved her to the door. Viv's mother always wanted her to play outside, and there it was, the invitation to do just that.

But Viv and J.J. hit it off immediately, score one for Viv's mom. J.J. introduced Viv to the other girls with the declaration, "I'm tired of being the only one that's not a teen yet. Now there will be two of us!"

That was several summers ago, and now, the moment Viv got to the summer house for vacation, she was on the phone with J.J.

"I'm back!"

And off they'd all go, pretty much every day and night. They rode bikes, swam at Libby's, ogled boys, and roller skated. Viv still had her book to read, but now she did it on the raft of the pontoon and traded paperbacks with Goldie every few days.

This particular day was all about trespassing. Mr. Ewald had a great rope swing but never let anyone on his property to use it.

Hope was the instigator on this one and decided that Ewald was keeping a Lake Manitou treasure to himself. "It's un-American!"

They all agreed, and now there they were, in the back of Ewald's place, deciding who was next into the water. Usually, J.J. wasn't so nervous. But they were trespassing on Mr. Ewald's lake frontage. Ewald had caught her once before.

"This one time, Ewald turned his hose on Jared and me. We were just walking through here to get to the public dock. It was freezing."

"You survived," Hope said.

"He's mean, and we were just walking," J.J. said.

Finally, Keith's head popped up from the water. "Okay, who's next?!!" He was treading water and waving them all in.

"I think I'll lose my suit!" Goldie was sporting a two-piece that did not look like it would survive a plunge into the lake at high velocity. But it was pretty.

"But it's the whole reason we came out here. Ugh, look, Hope and I can push. Who wants to try?" Libby and Hope were tall and had long arms. They'd be able to give the rope a good heave.

Viv wasn't usually the first to dive into trouble or adventure, but something came over her. They were here! It looked fun. And darn it, she'd show J.J. who the chicken was! She raised her hand like she was in class.

"Me! I'm doing it." Viv stepped forward. She kicked off her Keds and wiggled out of her cutoffs. She had her bathing suit under just about everything she wore in the summer.

Her mother had nagged her to wear a t-shirt today, even if she was swimming. Since she currently had blistered shoulders thanks to their ten hours on the raft over the weekend.

"Here, hold this too. I don't want Michael Hutchence to be damaged." She gave Goldie her shorts and her prized INXS t-shirt.

"Ducky," said Goldie.

"Okay, just hold on tight and let her rip when you get out there over the water," Libby said, instructing her on the fine art of hurling her body into the air.

Viv climbed into the disk. Both her feet fit better than Keith's did, but still, it was a tiny space.

"I'd not recommend a flip. Keith's good at that stuff," Hope cautioned her.

"Yeah, and don't forget to let go. You come flying back this way, and you're going to smack into the tree," said J.J.

"Quit scaring her. You'll be great, Viv. It's going to be fun," Libby said. Libby's confidence was catching. If Libby said you could do it; you could do it!

"I'm not scared." Viv wasn't. She was excited. Her mom would blow a gasket if she saw it, but her mom wasn't here.

"Hold on," Hope said.

Viv balanced on the little disc at the end of the rope and then gripped it tight.

Viv felt Libby and Hope pull her toward them and over a grassy bank that jutted into the water's edge. They kept pulling until the rope wouldn't stretch any further, and then they let loose. Viv held onto the rope but felt like she was flying.

She let out a hoot. It was so much fun! Her heart felt like it was flying too.

"Oh no!" Viv glanced toward her friends—they were running! What was happening? Why?

"Viv, LET GO!"

Keith was in the water below. He seemed frantic.

"NOW!"

She did as he said, and though she didn't have the skill to flip like Keith had, she soared anyway. For a second, she was in the air, still floating. And then she plunged into the lake. Taking a good amount of water up her nose.

She kicked up and broke the surface.

"Wow, that was boss!"

"We gotta swim for it."

"What?"

Keith pointed to the shore. There was Mr. Ewald, and he had a gun! He was pointing it at her friends as they ran like heck.

"It's a BB gun, but it can still shoot your eye out. We gotta swim."

"What about them?"

"They're headed for the public dock, off Ewald's spread."

She hoped none of them got hit with any BBs, and as she thought it, a pellet zipped past her.

"Come on!" Keith said again. They swam as fast as they could, out of range of Ewald's pellets. As they got closer to the public section of the beach, Keith stopped.

"You okay, Viv?"

"I'm great! That was great! We escaped!"

"You're a maniac," Keith said, and they swam, a little slower now, without the threat of losing an eye to one of old man Ewald's pellets.

Up ahead, Viv could see her friends waving them on. Laughing, also maybe crying. Basically, all the emotions raced through them with their adrenaline.

Viv's swing into the lake had turned into an adventure she'd never forget.

"Too bad we can't go again!" Viv said as she followed Keith toward the public beach.

Chapter Six

Viv

Viv looked out on Lake Manitou as she remembered the leap into that water. She hadn't hesitated. She hadn't worried about landing or smacking, as they called it, when you belly flop.

She'd barely worried about Old Man Ewald shooting her in the eyeball with a pellet!

Oh, to be young and not have every possible bad outcome play out like a horror movie in your mind.

She was all worry now. All caution. All fear.

"Where is she?"

Viv was pulled from her memory back to the sitting room of the hotel lobby. A wave of energy was rolling toward her in the form of her girlhood friends.

The memory of that long-ago day blurred into the present. Three women walked into the room, and it was easy to see who they were.

Hope. Her hair was still so enviably thick, but now a shock of white dominated it around her face. She was lean, and her arms looked strong. Her face was nearly free of makeup. The word natural described her. Beautifully natural. And she was so damn confident looking. Wow.

"Hope!" Viv stood up. Hope opened her arms and hugged her. Hope smelled like fresh lemon. She was a restauranteur now; they'd seen her place as they'd driven in. It looked warm, earthy, and beautiful. Viv just knew it would be like Hope herself.

And then J.J. practically leaped into the room.

"Get out of town! I can't even!!!" J.J. moved Hope aside and came in for her own hug.

"J.J.! You're kidding me. You look the same."

"Please." J.J. had a smile that changed her whole face. It lit it up. Her eyes danced, and her energy was the same as it had been when J.J., at eleven, had pronounced they were to be friends. She was compact and bouncy, like she'd been as a girl. Her hair now, though, was all layers and motion. Gone were the ponytails that used to bounce and flick. Viv just stared.

"It's true, though," Viv said. She wondered how she looked to them. She didn't have makeup on, not because she was into being natural, but mainly because she just didn't bother lately. Her hair was a disaster since the treatments. She felt a bit self-conscious all of a sudden.

Libby made up the caboose for the train of women. Goldie had star quality, but Libby had Queen Energy.

Truth be told, Libby was the woman in Viv's mind's eye when she designed some of her most popular Vivian Blackwood pieces. Younger Libby could have been a model in *Young Miss Magazine*, and she'd grown into the consummate woman in charge. She was the chic boss lady, even in this casual setting. Her air of authority scared billionaires and emboldened her friends when they were girls. If Libby was on your side, you were on the correct side.

"Stop, the gorgeousness of you," Viv said. Libby smiled at the compliment. She didn't deflect it away.

"You make it complete; we needed you," Libby said.

"What?"

"The Sandbar Sisters, we're all five here now, after all this time." Libby reached out a hand, and Viv took it. Libby squeezed it, but it was gentle. Viv appreciated this gesture. She was afraid another hug might send her into a crying jag. She was happy to see these faces. She didn't want to cry.

"Why has it been so long, really? That's a sin that it took thirty years," J.J. said.

"We had stuff to do, you know, finding husbands, getting rid of husbands, raising humans, starting businesses. But we got it now. We're all here," Libby said.

Viv wondered about the lives of these women. A lifetime ago, they shared their dreams. What do you want to be when you grow up?

Viv had always answered "mother" to that question, and then "artist."

She'd become both of those things, but not in the way she thought she would. The universe had different plans for her. But they were dreams fulfilled, nonetheless.

Her designs were her art. Her designs were her creative outlet.

"We know what you've been doing. Your designs are beautiful," Libby said.

"Darn right they are. She invented a category." Goldie knew Viv's story. She'd been a part of it. Goldie had even lobbied to wear all Vivian Blackwood Designs when she starred in Perfume Empire as a groundbreaking cosmetics CEO.

"Well, thank you. I had help. Speaking of that."

Siena walked into the scrum of women, and they went nuts over her. It was a bit of a relief for Viv. She moved away from the center of attention and tried to marshal her energy.

"We finally meet in person!"

Viv slowly realized Siena seemed to already know all her Sandbar Sisters.

Goldie came over and put her arm through Viv's.

"I told them about our family situation. I hope that is okay."

"Of course, it is."

Siena was Goldie's biological daughter.

When Goldie was pregnant by a big Hollywood player, she feared she couldn't keep her pregnancy away from the prying eyes of the Hollywood rumor mill. Viv had just had her fourth miscarriage. Goldie reached out to Viv, and it fell into place. It was like the universe wanted them both to be Siena's mother.

Viv's dream of motherhood came true, but also kept Goldie from becoming a Hollywood tragedy. They were a family.

But they'd kept it a secret at Goldie's insistence. Goldie had lied to protect a famous man and her own reputation, too. But Dustin Toms had only become more famous in the twenty-plus years Siena had been alive. Something had changed. Viv put the question to her.

"What's changed?"

"I realized I could trust these women; in a way I haven't found anywhere else. And now, our Siena has so many aunties."

"It looks like it, but what about...?" Viv was happy to see her daughter among her old friends. She'd need them. The idea that there would be a network of support comforted Viv and also stabbed into her heart.

"Yeah, he'll never find out because he has no reason to look," Goldie said it quietly. Siena had no idea who her biological father was. She had two moms, and two dads, more or less with Bret and eventually Travis. It was a small army of parental units. Why look for more? Viv hoped that was always the case.

Hope brought out lemonade and a tray of lovely morsels to nibble on.

"She calls them Nosh Plates at the restaurant. It's so cute I can hardly stand it," J.J. bragged about Hope. Hope shook her head in amusement.

"Hope's menu changes every week, always local, and you get what she makes, no menu of a million options," Libby said.

"I was lucky enough to have a dinner at The Lost Kitchen in Maine. She does that too! It's so amazing," Viv said. She'd had one of the best meals of her life at The Lost Kitchen.

"Yes, Erin French is my hero," Hope said.

"Well, you're *my* hero. This is so good," J.J. chimed in while enjoying a cracker spread with local cheese.

Viv wanted to love it too. But her appetite wasn't the same. Food didn't taste the same as it did before.

The food and drinks were arranged, and then the six of them worked on getting reacquainted. They weren't the same young girls; they'd all been through so much. Hope had just divorced a cheating husband and had two grown daughters. Hope's Table was the restaurant of her dreams, deferred for years, it turned out. The confidence Hope radiated was also newly won, it turned out.

"I guess I am lucky in that regard. My ex, Bret, he never stopped my desire to be a designer. In a lot of ways, he was the perfect partner, knew people, helped me get the line going years before I could have on my own."

"He sounds wonderful," Hope said.

"He is a great dad, too, right, Siena?"

"The best."

"If he hadn't been in love with Travis, maybe we'd still be married."

"Ah, gotcha," Hope said.

Then it was catching up with J.J. She worked at a local hair salon and was married to a man named Dean Tucker, who Libby referred to as a superhero. She had kids too, boys—well, men. Giant men, like their bear of a father, J.J. said.

"They're mostly civilized, but not entirely. I am always the odd woman out, so it's been such a nice thing having the Sandbar Sisters back! Helps me be less feral."

"Only a little less feral," Goldie said. And J.J. nodded in agreement.

Viv watched how comfortable the four of them were together

after all this time. Viv had that with Goldie but wondered if she could be close, again, to the other three. There was a literal lake between who she was before cancer and whoever she was now.

And then there was Libby. She was also coming out of a bad marriage.

"Yeah, I nearly got thrown in prison thanks to the fact that Henry's midlife crisis included felony embezzlement."

Viv remembered Henry. He was the rich one, the college one, that Libby had chosen over Keith. Their Keith. *What had happened to him*, she wondered.

"She never does anything halfway," Hope said about their friend. And Viv remembered that to be true. Libby was a leader, a crusader, and a take-the-bull-by-the-horns person.

"Just hearing about all you've done makes me want to take a nap," Viv said. She was serious. Libby was a force of nature.

"And you remember Keith Brady, well, they're a thing again," J.J. said.

Libby blushed.

Aha, well, there it was. Their Keith was still their Keith!

"Yes, who saw that coming?" Libby shrugged her shoulders.

"Anyone who ever saw you two back in the day," Viv said. She remembered heartthrob Keith and how he'd always treated their gaggle of girls with good humor. He was an honorary Sandbar Sister, but the driving force for that was clearly his love for Libby. It made her smile to think they'd wound up together. A happy ending, after all.

Libby had three kids, Viv learned, and from what Viv could see, she was still the leader of this little group, insomuch as she had a plan. She always had a plan.

Viv didn't realize until they started explaining Libby's plan how much she was supposed to be a part of it. When they started talking about the new Irish Hills, it was almost too much. Rehabbing an entire town? Viv didn't have the energy to curl her eyelashes, much less give a town CPR!

Viv sensed an energy shift in Siena. Her daughter was keyed up while the rest of them reminisced and laughed. Siena couldn't seem to sit still.

Viv saw Siena chew her fingernail. She never did that.

Finally, Siena stood up and spilled it.

"Mom, I know this will come as a shock to you, but, well, we're also a part of the new Irish Hills!"

"What?"

"We've leased the far end of the corner of buildings on Manitou Lake Road. We passed it on the way in, actually."

Viv had entrusted her finances to Siena. But she was having a tough time processing what her daughter was saying.

"Aunt Goldie hooked me up with Aunt Libby and let me know they needed a boutique. I mean, we're it. We're opening the very first Vivian Blackwood Designs retail location."

"I really don't understand the words coming out of your mouth right now."

"I want us to open a boutique in that space. I'll do the business end, of course, but it will be a possible proof of concept of Vivian Blackwood Boutiques across the country if it works. It's a new direction for the business, and it will help contribute to the rejuvenation that's happening here in Irish Hills."

Viv tried not to lose her temper. She saw the hope and youthful optimism in her daughter's eyes. But she wanted to go crawl into a bed, pull up the covers and stay there. She didn't want to start a new venture. Vivian Blackwood Designs was barely hanging on. She didn't have a new line of designs in her. That blank sketch book proved it.

"I don't have the energy. I thought we were relaxing. I'm feeling, what's the word?"

"Ambushed, I totally get it. I sort of felt that too, but I promise you this is going to cure what ails you. It did me," Goldie chimed in to defend Siena.

"What ailed you was a P.R. crisis. I have cancer." Viv knew it sounded mean; she regretted the tone as soon as it came out of her mouth.

Goldie came over and kneeled down in front of Viv. "Honey, I know. I know. No pressure, okay. Just forget all this. We are here to help you recharge, so let's just get you to your room. And we can talk about all this later." Goldie looked over her shoulder. Joe, who'd helped them in, nodded at Goldie.

"Okay, your stuff is already in your room."

"I don't mean to seem ungrateful; you all have good intentions, I get it. But I'm just not up for a new adventure, a new business. I'm barely up for showering each morning lately." Viv slumped in the chair. She felt a wave of emotion. She wanted to cry. She shouldn't cry. She was expected to be strong.

J.J. rushed to her and put her arms around Viv. And suddenly, she did cry. She let go, a little, of the burden of pretending like she was okay.

"You don't have to fake it here," J.J. said. "If you feel like crap, it's okay. You can feel like crap. You can tell us to go to hell. It's all allowed."

Viv smiled. There was an acceptance here, with her old friends. They were her age. Despite how anything looks on the outside, a woman in her fifties has been through some stuff, but she's survived. It isn't all sunshine and roses.

Sweet Siena, she was wonderful, but her daughter did look at the world as though everything would always work out. There would always be a fairytale ending. Because in Siena's life of twenty-three years, that had mostly been true.

"I'm sorry, Mom. I didn't want you to feel ambushed. I just, well, this is so exciting. I think I thought it would be the right thing to get you, uh, to make you..." Siena stopped.

"Honey, I understand, but starting a new business isn't on the list of self-care suggestions they gave us at the cancer center."

"This is long overdue, the boutique. We should have had one

in New York. And you are up for this. You heard Dr. Hinkley," Siena said.

"Yes, sure. I need to just rest. It was a long trip." Viv said. She wasn't in the mood to argue with her daughter in front of her friends. She'd give Siena a reality check later, in private. It wasn't something she wanted to do, crush her daughter's dreams. But a boutique? No. No way.

Goldie slid in to the rescue. "I'm going to show you to your room. You do not need to catch up with anyone anymore. Or start a business. Or anything. Come on."

Goldie had an arm around her.

"I don't mean to disappoint anyone."

"Stop, take a load off upstairs. The lake has a way of helping all of us get a good night's sleep," Libby said.

"The food was lovely, Hope."

"Thank you, love."

Goldie guided her away from the group.

"Siena has lost her mind," Viv said under her breath to Goldie.

"She means well. We all do."

"I know. I know."

"Here's the Vineyard suite. Everything you need. If there's something you want, just ring the front desk. My guy, Jaden's, back. He'll get anything to your room in mere seconds."

"Thank you, I am feeling a little, ugh. A boutique?" She shook her head again.

"Don't give it another thought. Rest, shower, do whatever. None of us are going anywhere."

"Was I too harsh with Siena?"

"Honey, our girl is tougher than one side-eye from you. She's fine."

Goldie left Viv to herself.

She looked around the room. It was lovely. Blonde wood floors, lavender paint on the walls, a painting of one of the huge lilacs that grew on the corner of the inn hung over the bed.

There was a comfy chair facing a huge window that looked out over the lake. Viv checkout out the bathroom, white tile floor and shower, and a claw-foot tub. Goldie had turned this into a feminine oasis. It was clean and uncluttered but also soft and peaceful.

Viv needed peace. She needed uncluttered. She was about to disappoint Siena and her old friends.

But then again, her own body had disappointed her. That was life.

Chapter Seven

Siena

"She did not seem so happy about that," Siena said.

Her new aunts were there, reassuring, cleaning up food, and finishing each other's sentences again. It was good to have their hub of activity. Their energy was upbeat, and after a year in cancer treatment waiting rooms, upbeat was a nice change.

But she was sick to her stomach after seeing her mother's reaction.

"I'm sure she'll be fine," J.J. said.

"Yeah, we pushed too hard. We tend to around here." Hope looked at Libby, who did not shrink with guilt, in Siena's estimation.

Goldie rejoined them.

"I blew it, Aunt Goldie."

"Nah, we were just a little fast. I didn't really understand how much she's still in recovery."

"I agree. She's trying to heal, and we dive-bombed her," Hope said.

"I'm not sure what to do next," Siena said.

Libby piped up.

"Your mom doesn't have to do a thing she doesn't want to do. But that doesn't mean you can't take a look at the space. The stock you ordered to start up has been delivered. You can get a feel for the space. You don't need Viv for that, right?"

"True. I mean, I know the line inside and out. And I'd love to maybe just set up something. Maybe it would be easier if she saw it all laid out. The heavy lifting, I can do that."

"You're just as creative as your mom and me and Bret! How could you not be?! That's a great idea. Set up the space." Goldie loved to brag about Siena. But bragging from a parent did not magically make a person talented. Siena was talented. She'd just been in a lot of shadows when it came to her moms and dad. "It's settled. You are going to catch some rays. Maybe use the paddle board out there for the rest of today. Just do whatever you want, and tomorrow you and Libby will see the store," Aunt Goldie had decreed the rest of the day's events. That was that.

A day to relax at the lake sounded great. But then Libby quietly reminded her of the promise she'd made.

"You signed the lease. The bad news is that I have spent the deposit. No matter what you decide, the space is yours for a year." That eliminated the idea of scraping this entire idea. An idea she thought was brilliant only a few minutes ago.

"Okay," Siena said.

"I'm going to show you your room. It's a totally different floor than your mom's. You're going to take a break from taking care of her. Leave that to us. Let us take care of the both of you." Goldie, the diva, was playing Goldie, the earth mother. Siena was happy to let go of the reins for a while. Relieved even.

"That's sweet, thank you. I know there are things that would be easier for her to share with a friend than a daughter."

"Exactly, she doesn't want you to worry. We got it. It's a mom thing. Seriously, there are fun things to do here, even hot young guys," J.J. said, and Hope smacked her on the arm. "Hey, what? I'm married, not dead."

Siena laughed and relaxed a bit. The women all seemed ready to handle anything. For the last year, Siena had been in that role.

"And tomorrow afternoon, it's a trip downtown. I think you'll be inspired. You'll see the future," Libby predicted.

Okay, that was a plan. She could do that, chill a little. Maybe sit out on the big dock outside. The hot guy part of the plan seemed unlikely. She didn't need that, really. She needed to save Vivian Blackwood Designs.

The ladies said their goodbyes. Goldie showed her to her room.

It was a nod to a sixties kind of mid-mod vibe.

"This is what so many cabins and cottages looked like when I grew up here."

"Oh my gosh, Eames chairs? And an original Steelcase desk? Come on, Aunt Goldie, you're too much." It all looked groovy, sleek, and so very what Siena would have picked herself!

"I had you in mind the whole time I was furnishing this room. And darling, you know me, I just cannot be surrounded by ugly décor!"

"I know, I know. Is it okay if I explore, and all that, around the grounds?"

"Do whatever floats your boat. I have some calls, a few emails, and one more guest check-in for the day. Oh, the WiFi password is over by the desk if you need it."

"Thanks."

Goldie saluted her and then shut the door.

This had to work. Siena had run out of ideas. Her mother had trusted her with the business during the cancer treatment, and it was failing. She was failing.

Siena had to succeed.

Chapter Eight

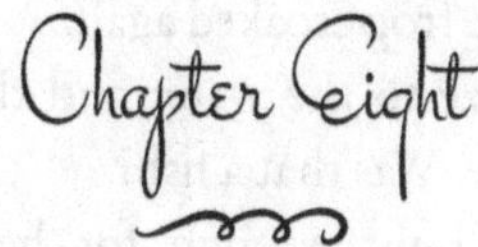

Viv

Viv woke once in the night. It wasn't to take medication or because stark terror pushed her into the scariest parts of her mind.

It was frogs.

She had left the door open to the small Juliet balcony off her room. Maybe it was the night breeze that feathered over the uneven hairdo she'd grown back that gently nudged her awake. But the loud croak of frogs kicked in and finished the job of interrupting her sleep. The frogs were a symphony of amphibian romance.

It was warm out, especially for early in the season, and the frogs were under the impression they lived in the swamps of Louisiana. Did they not know this was Michigan?

Viv swung her feet on to the thick area rug Goldie had selected for this pretty room. It felt good, and it eased her body from drifting dreams to standing solidly on her feet.

She walked out onto the little balcony and let the sounds of late spring serenade her. The water lapped on the dock below. The hoot of an owl let her know it was close, looking for a late-night snack, maybe.

"If you're smart, there's a frog or two you could nosh on," Viv instructed the unseen owl.

As if in protest, the frog croaked again.

She shifted her gaze to the water and the big dock. A splash broke the glassy surface. Was that a fish?

The moon was bright enough for her to figure out that someone was swimming. It may be warm, but the lake still had to be so cold. Who'd be nutty enough to swim in the dark?

Viv watched. It was a man. He had a good strong stroke as he swam parallel to the beach. He did three or so laps and then waded over to the sandy part of the shore.

Viv felt a little strange, spying, but then again, it wasn't like a private beach or something. She was just standing on her balcony. The man was in shape, and that was pretty clear. She remembered what it was like to care if she was shaped a certain way. She did not anymore. Her healthy body was a thing of the past. Fretting over whether she had abs or slimmer thighs had wasted so much time in her life. It made her ashamed to think about the shallow preoccupations of her younger self.

That was another thing. She'd designed clothes for women that looked like Libby. Nobody looked like Libby.

Had she made people worry about their own bodies? She hoped not. She'd aimed to empower women, but maybe she'd done the opposite. Using the long, lean lines of the Libbys of the world didn't help the J.J.s.

The man toweled off, and what was that? Something out of place on the beach caught her eye. A metal pole glinted in the moonlight. What?

Viv realized the man hopped over to it, and she saw now he was using a crutch. As fast as he had been swimming, his gate on land was awkward and unsteady. He was recovering from some injury.

She watched as he struggled up the incline toward the back of the hotel.

And then he looked up. She slid back into the shadow of the building. Shoot. Had he seen her? Was she now the old lady creeper?

Ugh, she hoped not.

Viv walked back into her room. She turned the light on in the bathroom. She looked at herself in the mirror. Her hair was back. It was different. All white now. But it had come back thicker. It had no shape. It was just back, a weird misshapen blob. Maybe she could have J.J. cut it, some cute, sassy cut, something like J.J. herself had?

She ran her hand through her hair. She speculated that losing all the over-processed locks was an unintended benefit of her recent health hell?

Viv was pale. She thought of her sunburned summers here. Did that click on the cancer cells in her body? Or was the cancer just a genetic gift from her mom?

Not for the first time, she thanked God that Siena was her heart's daughter, not her body's. She could put aside worries that she'd passed along bad genes.

Siena.

She was so excited about the boutique idea. A retail location for the Vivian Blackwood line of clothes? Viv hadn't been able to design one new piece in months. And now Siena was trying to expand into this new direction. This just wasn't where Viv wanted to expend what energy she had. Opening a store and trying to save the sinking ship that was Vivian Blackwood Designs was probably futile. It would certainly require a full-tilt effort from her and from Siena. Viv had to say no. She'd have to be firmer with her daughter.

Viv Blackwood was out of ideas, but more than that, she was out of time.

If the last year had taught her anything, it was that. But this trip had shown her Siena was just starting. She deserved to live a new adventure. Siena shouldn't be so tied to Viv's dreams, to Viv's past.

Viv crawled into bed and closed her eyes. Slowly her mind cleared. She'd been working on pushing away the worst thoughts. At least some of the positive thinking crap was valid.

She drifted into a night of sleep. She dreamed of diving off the raft. She dreamed of slicing through the water with her strong arms.

She dreamed of being whole.

Chapter Nine

Siena

Siena rose early. She had the best night of sleep she'd had in a while.

They weren't kidding about the lake air.

She didn't wake up her mom. If she was sleeping well, it was best to let her. Goldie assured her that if Viv needed anything, it would be Goldie that would handle it.

It was sweet to see her movie star mom being so humble, to see her enjoying serving and caretaking. She wondered what the people of Irish Hills thought about Oscar Winner Goldie Hayes picking up her matcha tea powder at the local grocery store.

It made her smile. Maybe they were used to it by now.

Siena showered and made her way down to the Two Lakes Hotel lobby. It really was her Aunt Goldie to a T. Glamour wasn't a thing. It was a vibe. Goldie had that vibe, whether it was her fancy mansion in California or this historic hotel in Michigan. She made a place twinkle.

Siena walked past the check-in counter and outside. The

morning air was crisp. She took a deep breath in. The lake air was different, summery. Siena would have a busy summer even if all this did go to plan.

Libby drove up in a vintage Jeep Wrangler. Libby wore a crisp white t-shirt tucked into distressed jeans, but a navy-blue linen blazer pulled it all together. Libby Quinn was in charge. Siena would not have guessed Jeep Wrangler for this woman, but Aunt Libby was right at home behind the wheel as they drove downtown.

Libby was a formidable person. Siena had Googled her, and sure, the business of the bad husband and scandal came up. But if you looked beyond that six-month period where her life fell apart, every other swing Libby Quinn Malcolm made was a home run.

She had met U.S. presidents thanks to her work. She'd met Bono! Her efforts in rehabbing communities and neighborhoods had been recognized internationally, and yet here she was, focusing on Irish Hills.

Siena decided to start there with her questions.

"So, what was Bono like?"

Libby laughed. "Oh, well, I didn't hang with him for very long. It was an award thing. But he was charming, soft-spoken, sexy, and way too short for me. I had three-inch heels on."

She'd met a few celebrities when visiting Aunt Goldie, but in her opinion, Aunt Goldie outshone them all. She also knew what it was like to be taller than most dudes when she wore heels.

"I've never seen Aunt Goldie like this. She's just straight up happy and totally in control of her path."

"I would say that the pressure of Hollywood is intense. She's calling her own shots now. There is a lot to be said for that. Also, a lot is to be said for not having all that pressure not to age or show signs of aging. I mean, I'm not a fan of my wrinkles, but I also don't get fired for having them."

Siena looked out the Jeep window. The lake peeked out between cottages.

There was a vibe here. She couldn't put her finger on it. It was relaxed on the one hand, but also a frisson of excitement ran through her. It was like finding hidden treasure.

They pulled into downtown, and people were out and about already, riding bikes and bustling in and out of the mercantile on the main drag and the grocery store down the street. Siena could already see there was untapped potential here for a retail experience. She was determined to create that experience with Vivian Blackwood Designs Boutique.

"Here we are. Let's go into the space. Have you taken a look?"

Libby was so accomplished, like her mom and Aunt Goldie. Siena didn't want to disappoint any of them or fall short. She paused. She wanted to charge ahead, but her mother's reaction put a damper on things.

"I'm trying to save mom's business, but mom too." The realization of her true motives spilled out of her; she hadn't planned to say that. She really barely knew Libby.

Libby stopped. She dropped her cool business-like demeanor. She took a breath.

"There's nothing wrong with that."

"It's just the light is gone, the business needs help, but, well, mom just isn't the same after all she's been through."

"And why would she be? But she's still Viv. I am sure of it."

Libby put a hand on Siena's shoulder, and Siena nodded in agreement. But she didn't really know if she believed that her mom would be okay.

"It's okay. We all want to help her and give you a little breather too. You're going to make this work, and we'll help you take care of your mom. It's going to work out. I just know it will. Come on."

Siena had just met Libby, but she felt reassured by her. Libby's certainty that Siena was moving in the right direction helped her stand up straighter. She lifted her chin. Maybe this wasn't the disaster it seemed to be. Maybe there was some way to make this work.

She opened her eyes to the possibility of a bright future right here, in this summer town.

Siena was struck again by how adorable the main street was. This was Libby's doing, but Hope's restaurant had also helped turn Irish Hills into this stylish gem.

Irish Hills was the "in" place for country music stars when they didn't want to be seen but also did want to be seen. That was Aunt Goldie's contribution. Her star power was strong enough to lure other celestial bodies. It was just a touch of glamor that had put Irish Hills on the map.

All of that had helped convince Siena that her plan had been right. She loved the idea of her mom building something here. She just had to convince her mom.

Hope's Table was red brick, and the building wrapped around the corner. There was a clear view in the back of the restaurant toward the lake. Siena imagined having a meal with the lake view. A white brick two-story space next to the restaurant displayed a *For Rent* sign in the window. Then a longer lower structure stretched down the block with huge store front windows. A striped awning announced it as the Irish Hills Mercantile. Next to the Mercantile was another available retail space. At the far end, creating a book end to Hope's Table on the block, sat the proposed space for Vivian Blackwood Boutique.

"It's so darn cute. The spaces are just gorgeous and historic but not cookie-cutter. Wow. Are these buildings, the way they look different but charming, your influence?" Siena asked Libby.

"I was the big picture gal, and I know how to get great people to join me." Libby raised her eyebrows at Siena. As though she thought Siena was a great person. That was nice, but right now, Siena felt like she'd fumbled. Big time.

They parked in the front of the space Siena had committed to taking for the Vivian Blackwood Shop. Siena looked down the row toward the other end, where Hope's restaurant anchored the block.

"Are you sure about us taking this anchor end? Maybe those two smaller spaces, with the lease signs?"

"No, I've got ideas for them. You're the anchor. I have this feeling you're going to need the space."

Siena couldn't help imaging what the store could be. She stopped second-guessing the plan and let Libby's enthusiasm set the tone. Siena's mind raced over the inventory, the best sellers of Vivian Blackwood Designs, and how they would use them to fill the store.

"Our big seller was this scarf and shawl combo that works on a deck or a cruise or as a throw on your couch. I can see that selling here too." Siena knew the product line. She'd taken photos for social, curated customer photos, and even helped model pieces her mom designed. But where a lot of girls would love the modeling aspect, Siena liked to see the whole picture. She loved watching her mom's design process and learned the business of fashion merchandising from her dad. Bret Blackwood knew how to market a brand. That's what her mom always said.

Siena had so much to live up to.

"Okay, so welcome to the space." Libby opened the door.

A little bell hit the arm of the hinge. A musical little tinkle greeted customers as if this was an old general store. The space here, though, was open. It was light, obviously restored with an eye to keeping the character of the old building. You could feel the place, hoping for a dream to fill the space. Well, Siena could, anyway.

Anywhere else, Siena would guess that the floors were reproductions or reclaimed from somewhere, but to her eye, they looked original. If they weren't, Dean Tucker had done a terrific duplicate. The front door was centered between two display windows. They could display something gorgeous from her mom's line. Ooh, what would be best? Siena thought of her mom's current offerings and wondered how new pieces could be featured in a way to draw people from the sidewalk into the space.

"It's a huge rectangle, really," Siena said.

"Yes, a blank canvas."

Siena walked the space. She turned around.

"You've got a restaurant, a mercantile. What are they selling?" Siena wanted to get into the mindset of the shoppers.

"Irish Hills Mercantile has gourmet groceries items, stuff the grocery store doesn't stock. They do pots and pans, some t-shirts, they've got a little souvenir section. Some of the ingredients, local produce, and local cheese that Hope uses are in the Mercantile. They're trying to keep things in stock that you might need if you're renting for the summer. You know, you're there and don't have a corkscrew or something. Between that, the hardware store and Barton's Food Village, the basics are handled. You're the next level of retail experience."

Siena also knew the restaurant scene was booming.

"I can't wait to try Aunt Hope's restaurant."

"Oh, and there's a new diner across town; they've got really tasty family fare there if you can't get into Hope's. I'm trying to get an investor to reopen Tut's Place, an old ice cream stand we used to have. That's on my to-do list for this year and maybe next year if I can't get to it."

"What about a bakery?"

"The gas station bakes donuts, But I'm still working luring a full service bakery. Maybe across the street. With a coffee shop. That stretch of buildings is in the long-term plan."

"Yeah, that would be a fantastic addition."

"Agree. I'm trying to do it with local or small entrepreneurs. Our lakes don't have sharks, so I'm trying to make sure our businesses don't either."

"And people are renovating houses all over Lake Manitou."

"Yes, it's nuts. I mean hot, hot, hot, even though the real estate market nationally has cooled down. Thanks to all the work we're doing, Irish Hills is on the upswing."

Siena was getting excited. "I think I know what you need to add to downtown."

"What? I'm adding you!"

"Yeah, but a hip home décor boutique, that would be a nice complement to our clothing store."

"What? I hadn't even thought of that."

"Think about it, you grab your coffee, you try on some of mom's designs, and wander across the way for a cool painting or vase or whatever for your new lake home."

"Do you know anyone who does that? I think you're on to something."

"Ha, no, just thinking out loud. I think I'm going to have my hands full getting Mom on board. I have to make it easy. She's been through so much." Siena needed to focus on fashion and not all the other ideas that might work here in Irish Hills.

Libby got her back on track as they moved to the back of the rental space. "Hmm. Well, some of the stuff you had shipped here has arrived already. In the back, past that door, we have storage, a space that could be an office, and even a little conference room or break room for staff. Whatever you need."

"Great! Let's see what's here." Siena had ordered the basics to start the store. Maybe if she staged it just a bit, it would be easier for her mom to get on board. She had to fire her mother's innate creativity somehow.

Libby gave Siena the rest of the tour of the space, and as they were done, they got serious. This was serious.

"This is your space, but you know, there is one caveat to all this."

Siena did know. She'd agree to it. "Your deadline."

"Right, I get that your mom is an obstacle, sort of, that you didn't anticipate." Siena had agreed to get the store open by June 15th, right before the start of the big summer rush. She didn't think it would be a problem, but now, with her mother's rejection of the idea, it seemed like a major problem.

"I have enough inventory to start the store, even if she is slow to warm up."

"You're not dealing with a cold corporate robot. First and foremost, I love your mom and want what's best for her and you. But I made promises here, to thousands of people in this town, to the people that own businesses too, that I'd make Irish Hills a success. It's their livelihood. Do you see?"

"I do."

"If you can't do this, really can't, or it's not the right time, I need to find something else. Fast." Libby was in the same position as Siena, really. She'd made promises. People depended on her. And she was depending on Siena for this piece of the puzzle.

Siena wasn't going to let this idea fail. She'd promised Aunt Libby, and she knew her mother would rally. A store here was going to work. She'd make sure of it.

"Vivian Blackwood Designs will not let you down. I promise."

Libby hugged her and then left her with the keys. They made plans to meet at Hope's for lunch.

Siena would figure this out. Her mom would snap out of it. And this would be a success. It just had to be.

Chapter Ten

Viv

Viv had slept well.

She woke up late. She felt rested, not drugged. The haze of the last few months often meant she slept only to awaken and feel worse.

She inhaled deeply. The white curtains with scalloped edges fluttered in the window. The sun streaming in put her in a different place, a different time.

For a moment, she let her mind slip to a time when that daylight and that smell meant it was going to be a great day on the raft. When she had no reason to fear the day or the future. When she couldn't wait to get to the water.

Viv would try to hold onto that outlook today. There didn't have to be a dark cloud. She didn't need to be the dark cloud.

Viv pulled on a loose skirt and tunic, along with her favorite flip-flops. These days she couldn't stand to be even remotely uncomfortable when it came to clothes. She'd cared less and less about coordinating her look and more and more about moving without pain or binding or chafing.

She wandered into the lobby closer to lunch than breakfast.

A young guy manning the lobby introduced himself. "Hi, I'm Jaden. We've got a lunch spread out in the dining room for our guests. If there's something else that seems more appealing. I can get it for you."

Jaden was tall, thin, and had A Flock of Seagulls type asymmetrical hair situation. He had to be over eighteen but didn't look it.

"Jaden, thank you, I'm sure it's all wonderful."

"We've got iced tea, lemonade, soda pop, whatever you'd like. I can bring it out to the veranda if you'd like to enjoy lunch with our best view."

"I would love some coffee and a little ice water. Does that work?"

"Sure does." Jaden put out an arm so Viv could enter the dining room. She hadn't had an appetite lately, but the lake air, the late hour, and who knows what else had fired up her hunger. Dr. Hinkley would be so proud.

She put a chicken salad croissant, some grapes, and a few pieces of cheese on her plate.

Jaden wasn't lying. The veranda was screened in, but it didn't inhibit the view. Lake Manitou stretched out before her. It wasn't crowded yet. It was serene. But there were a few boats, one or two small ones, sitting in the water, hoping for fish. A pontoon floated slowly by, waving to a few guests sitting on the lawn. Viv had the urge to paint the scene.

She regretted not having her sketch book.

She smiled. She wanted to paint? Her creative side had been dormant for the last few months. She'd had no desire to sketch. Nothing had felt worthy of her time. But just now, a little ping, just like she used to have. She shook her head. She recognized when she needed to express herself after a lifetime of manifesting her imagination into something real.

Jaden found her with the coffee and water. She sat on a comfy Adirondack chair and used a little side table next to her. She felt lighter inside. It was a bit unfamiliar. Waking up in a good mood, without having to marshal "good vibes," was not her life these days.

Maybe it was best not to question that. It was best to just try to enjoy it.

Viv took a deep breath. She savored the buttery croissant, and she inhaled the aroma of the coffee. This was it. This was the way to peace: fluffy pastry.

Without cynicism, she actively directed her mind to work the techniques they'd been aiming at her in her cancer support group. She was in the moment. Siena would be so proud.

"Ah, there she is. The creeper!"

The loud, male voice cut through her moment of attempted Zen.

She spilled a bit of coffee on her shirt and cursed under her breath.

And then the body attached to the loud voice ambled directly in front of her view.

It was the man from last night. He had one crutch and the boot she'd seen. And he had a big smile on his face. It was charming, despite his obnoxious comment.

"Do I know you?" she asked.

He leaned forward and tilted an ear toward her.

She repeated her question. "I said, do I know you?'

"You know what I look like in the moonlight, darling. What more is there to know?"

Viv took a breath. She needed to defend herself. She hadn't planned to be a Peeping Tom. It just happened. "I'm not a creeper! I just happened to be out on the balcony, and you were there, showing off."

He laughed. "You got me pegged immediately. I *am* a showoff."

Viv had not expected to win this exchange so quickly. She also did not want to be in this exchange, or any actually, with this stranger.

Viv hadn't noticed the other night, but along with the broken left leg, he had what looked like a few fresh scars on the left side of his face. She tried not to stare at them but instead met his eyes. His eyes were happy. The light brown color matched the reddish hair. He had a little stubble that was most definitely gray. He had the abs of a younger man but was no spring chicken, she decided.

"I'm Larson Taggert." He crutched over, hopped on one foot as he arranged his balance, and put out his right hand to shake.

"I'm trying to just be alone here, have lunch."

"Sure, sure, but I crutched all the way over. That's an effort. At least tell me your name?"

Viv decided it was best to comply with the man's desire to be sociable. She did not feel like making new friends. She was knee-deep in trying to navigate her old friends on this strange trip. But maybe if she introduced herself, he'd be happy and go away.

"My name's Vivian."

"Nice to meet you! Now, I'll know how to address you the next time you spy on me," he winked with the eye that seemed like it escaped the cuts on his face, but just barely.

"I said I wasn't—"

Just then, Jaden interrupted their burgeoning bickering. "Mr. Taggert, your staff is here."

"I told you to call me Tag, and it's my crew, not staff. They'll revolt if they hear you call them that."

"Sorry, Mr. Tag, uh, Tag. Your crew is here."

Whoever they were, Viv was glad he had somewhere else to go.

"Catch you later, Vivian." He rearranged himself on the crutches and mumbled a curse or two at the devices as he headed out, presumably to meet "the crew."

Viv turned around to watch him crutch off toward the front of the hotel.

"I know you're looking!" He turned rather quickly for a man on crutches and caught her again.

She whipped her head back around. What an infuriating person! She refocused on her lunch and tried to forget meeting Larson Taggert.

Back to the issue of the day: her daughter's youthful optimism that now, of all times, was the right time to open up a boutique of Vivian Blackwood Designs.

They'd always sold to high-end department stores and direct to wealthy clients, but they'd never been in the retail store management business.

Viv sat a while.

The warm air and lake breeze called to her.

If she was here, she should take advantage of the place. She could mull over the way to handle Siena just as well outside as inside.

Viv walked out the porch screen door and out onto the grounds.

She remembered this place from her childhood. It was clearly fancy now and stunning. But back then, it was kind of hulking. It had been fitted and refitted many times over by the time Goldie got here. But Goldie had put her movie-star money and style into this renovation, and it showed. Gone was any mismatch or haphazard add-on.

Viv walked out to the lawn that faced the lake. Every blade of grass on this property now was intentional. That was the word. It wasn't overly fussy or planted. It was landscaped with native plants that gave way to lake stones that provided a border out to the beach.

A huge dock proved space for boats and for sun bathers. A row of lounge chairs neatly lined up at the edge of the beach provided a place to sit and watch whatever lazy lake happenings were underway.

Viv spied a peddle-boat. She wondered if she had the lung

capacity for that. That would be fun, peddling around the lake, not too far, but just a little exploration. Although...she could easily see herself stuck out in the lake, drifting endlessly as her weak-as-a-kitten body helplessly waited for rescue.

Ugh. She hated being like this.

Viv decided she needed a little rest. She'd dealt with a stranger, had breakfast, and taken a little stroll. That was enough. The lounges were the perfect place to sit, just for a bit. The small hill back up to the inn looked too big all of a sudden. She wasn't expected anywhere. She sat down in the reclining chairs and felt her limbs grow heavy.

Just a little rest.

"Mom."

Siena's voice was gentle. It eased her out of the best nap of her life.

Viv looked down, and someone had covered her with a light blanket.

"What the heck, what time is it?"

"It's three in the afternoon. You've been napping, Aunt Goldie said, for three hours!"

"Oh, wow, ugh, what?" Viv shook off the disorientation of losing all that time. But she felt surprisingly alert now, awake.

"She covered you with the blanket and kept checking on you to be sure a goose didn't decide to poo on ya," Siena said and then sat next to her on the adjacent lounge.

"I guess I needed it. I swear that was the best rest I've had in ages. What an old lady."

"You're healing,

"Let's hope." Viv watched as Siena bit her nail again.

Siena was anxious. Viv could see that. Viv felt a stab of guilt. She'd made her daughter anxious. Her cancer, and her reaction yesterday to this business idea, both of them had turned her normally even keel girl into someone who bites her fingernails.

Viv tried to open her mind a little beyond the word "no" when it came to the future. She had spent her entire parenting life protecting Siena, and this year she'd dropped the ball. She couldn't even see the ball.

She changed the subject from rest or talk of healing.

"So, you went into town. How was the space?" Viv didn't want to encourage this idea of a boutique, but her desire to see her daughter was stronger than her reticence about the plan.

Siena lit up at the question.

"Mom, you need to see it! Downtown Irish Hills is the cutest ever, and it's all just getting started. And the space is, it's everything we'd need. It's got a huge opportunity for display in the windows, at the sidewalk--oh, it's even got adorable office space in back we could both use to work. Libby even suggested a little break room, too. I like that. The floor, the floor, is to die for. It's something we'd put in ourselves, except it's already there!"

"Ah, sounds lovely." And it did. Viv was sure Libby had done things right with whatever renovations she oversaw in Irish Hills, or anywhere for that matter.

"And we could be a part of something, of the town, you know? They have little parades, and they go nuts around North of Nash."

"North of Nash?"

"Oh, yeah, it's North of Nash, as in Nashville. It's this huge country music festival up the road at the racetrack. Aunt Libby said thanks to Aunt Goldie, the country stars just swarm the place in the summer."

"Ah, okay." Viv was trying to keep up with her daughter's speedy delivery of the virtues of Irish Hills.

"And we'd fit in, I think, really well. We'd really add to the reason people are coming here. Plus, I love the idea of helping to revitalize a town. It's a mission, you know? The town grows, and we grow Vivian Blackwood Designs."

"There's not much to grow. You know that sales are not great. I mean, that's my fault for not having anything new."

"Oh, that's why we're here, to be new!"

Viv couldn't help but smile at the light in Siena's eyes. She was excited, keyed up for the future, and bursting with ideas. If only that optimism was contagious.

"Honey, I love that you're excited. I do. I want to be too, but I just don't have the energy yet." She added the yet as though, at some future date, Viv would be energized. She didn't see that happening, but she also didn't want to crush the dreams of her sweet girl. Yet. Or ever. She left it unsaid.

"I want you to be better, to rest, to get stronger. I don't want to push you too hard. Not after all you've been through, but how about this: I do all of it. I set up the store, staff it, stock it, all the things. You do what you're a genius at, and that's design the new line."

"I don't know about genius." Viv put her hand out, and Siena took it in hers. Siena's fingers were long and tapered. Viv's were stronger and shorter, the veins in her hands looking ropey to her own eyes.

"You are, mama, you are. But there's no need for you to do too much. I will get this store going. And you can work and rest to suit how you're feeling."

Viv had said no. She'd been unequivocal about it. Siena's eyes sparkled, and her body radiated with energy and possibility. It had been a year of Siena doing everything to keep Viv on track with treatments and appointments. Her daughter needed something to look forward to that wasn't her mother's cancer treatment or support meeting and worse.

Viv didn't have the heart to say no again. She did not want to design a new line. She did not want to open a store that featured her career-minded fashion. She just wanted to—

She stopped. Viv didn't know what she wanted to do other than go back upstairs to the elegantly quiet room and stick her head under the covers.

However, her drive to make sure her daughter was happy was stronger than anything else. Viv took a breath, looked down at her body, the one she didn't recognize, and then back at Siena's hopeful expression.

And she caved.

"Okay, you take the lead at the store. I'll get out my sketch book and do my best."

"YES!" Siena jumped up and kissed Viv on the cheek.

Viv laughed as Siena then did a completely dorky happy dance.

Goldie happened to be walking down to the beach as Siena did her knee-knocking move.

"Wait, is this for TikTok?" Goldie said.

"No, no, just celebrating. Mom's back!" Siena said, and Goldie high-fived her.

Viv was not back. But despite that, she laughed. She shook her head. "Oh, brother, what have I gotten myself into?" Viv said.

For a moment, Siena's optimism really was contagious. She'd help Siena with her dream even though her own dreams were in the rear view.

Chapter Eleven

Siena

With her mother's blessing, Siena could go full speed ahead. And she did. There was not a moment she wasn't planning something for the store.

She'd decided the store's aesthetic would mimic her mother's clean and professional designs. Racks of crisp white tailored shirts would pop against the brick walls of the store. Her mom's signature line of pencil skirts in classic colors would be on round racks in the middle of the store floor. Siena had ordered hooks to display the array of flattering blazers on the walls. Siena had planned this well. They had plenty of merchandise from last year's line to start the store.

While her mother was set up on the porch of Two Lakes Grove with her sketch book and the lake as inspiration, Siena was unpacking boxes, searching for display tables, and wondering for the millionth time if they should change out the lighting in the space.

There was a lot to do to meet Aunt Libby's deadline.

Designing labels, hiring a couple of part-time sales associates, and figuring out an inventory tracking system left her little time for anything else.

Siena worked non-stop and loved it. Almost anything she needed, Aunt Libby and Aunt J.J. could point her in the right direction to find. And when she forgot to have lunch, it would appear via Aunt Hope and her waitress, Lila Pawlak.

Lila, Siena learned, was Aunt J.J.'s niece. Her dad owned Peck's Hardware Store. The small-town connections tickled Siena. She'd never experienced that in the big city life Bret and her mom had lived.

And it was accurate to say that Aunt J.J.'s husband, Dean, was a superhero like Aunt Libby said. He'd met her at the store this morning and helped her install a chandelier to replace the track lighting that had come with the space.

She had tried to do it on her own and realized too late that it was a two-person job.

"Okay, give it a go!" Dean told her from the ladder. He showed her the main fuse box and explained what each switch controlled. She turned the main electricity back on. He flipped the light switch, and the crystal chandelier glowed to life.

"OOH! It works!" she said as Dean remained up on the ladder. The lighting was key. It had changed the game inside the store.

"The height of this okay? We can make it higher, lower?"

"I think it's perfect."

"I think so too, and way better than that track lighting I had. You've got good taste."

"Uh, you're the one who restored these floors. I'd say you do too."

"Do not tell your Aunt J.J. that. She likes to say I'm part grizzly bear."

Siena saw that too, but only because Dean Tucker was grizzly-sized.

Ooh, another idea lit up in Siena's mind. She made a note to herself as Dean whistled in appreciation at how the new light changed the look of the store.

"You're good at décor. This made a huge difference."

"Thank you, right? It just really looks perfect."

"Now, I'm told if you do not go to Hope's for lunch, the Sandbar Sisters will invade this space and unleash a whirlwind of nagging."

"Oh, can you let them know that I have to skip? I just had an idea, and I don't have time for eating out."

"I will not. My wife scares me. I try to stay on her good side." Dean smiled.

The idea of this big mountain of a man being afraid of the little dynamo that was Aunt J.J. was adorable.

"Okay, okay. I'll go. I, too, am afraid of Aunt J.J."

"I'll lock up. You walk over right now and also give me full credit for insisting that you get lunch."

"I shall. You're the reason I'm going. Check."

"Good."

"And Dean, thank you again for the help. I just love the light fixture."

"No problem at all, but don't try electrical without me again. Okay? I need to be able to sleep at night without worrying that you're zapping yourself over here."

"Yes, sir."

Siena grabbed her bag and took the short walk over to Hope's Table. The place was filled with lunch diners. Aunt Hope was at her gorgeous French stove, involved in the hypnotic choreography of shifting cast iron pans and sliding in and out of the kitchen traffic. It was part of the experience, Siena realized, watching an artist in her element.

J.J. waived Siena over to a table where Libby and an older woman sat as well. Apparently, it was four for lunch. Truth be told, Siena wanted to skip lunch and work the store, but she now had four new mother hens worrying over her.

"Siena! This is my Aunt Emma, the Queen of Irish Hills if there ever was one."

"I prefer Empress."

The older woman put out a hand, and Siena shook it gently. Aunt Emma was stylish, over-dressed even, but looked very, very elderly to Siena.

"I'm pleased to meet you."

"And you, you have the most gorgeous qualities of Goldie without the, how do they say it these days, vertical challenges?"

So, it appeared the cat was out of that bag. She was quiet about Aunt Goldie, but all these women had Aunt Goldie's trust.

"Don't worry, I've kept bigger secrets than that."

Libby rolled her eyes. "She's not lying."

J.J. chimed in.

"I'm starving. Hope has a Michigan Cherry Salad for lunch today. It sounds too light. It is light, but trust me, it's the best salad you'll ever have."

They ordered, and soon the conversation turned to how the shop was going.

"I'm excited," Siena told them "I've got a good amount of product to start us out, Mom's designs from last season, but she's onboard with coming up with something new too. I don't think she's up to a full line, just a few new pieces we can feature at the store. We can even call them exclusive since they're not in the department stores yet. We're going to be in good shape."

"Career wear?" Aunt Emma said. There was a strange edge to her voice.

"Yes, that's the Hallmark of Vivian Blackwood Designs. A new piece or two on display here, and we probably can get some fashion magazine coverage too."

"That's great," Libby said.

"So, get me up to speed for the season, my dear," Aunt Emma said.

"We're going well!" Libby reported. "Hope's is firing on all cylinders well in advance of the start of the busy season. We've got the mercantile going, and the upgrades at Arrow's Gas station and the Two Lakes Grove Hotel are pretty much done. That's a lot of what I promised. And what will be on the update to the town council."

Siena knew Libby had pushed developers away from Irish Hills, and she'd also secured a grant for all the renovations in the very building they sat in, and the space Siena was renting. It was impressive. She could learn a lot from Libby, from all her new "aunts."

But for now, they were right. She was starving.

Luckily, just then, Lila popped over, said hello, and put their lunch selections in front of them. Siena dug in.

"And this summer, we'll be prepared for your country music superstar invasion. I won't have to hawk my wares," Aunt Emma said.

"No, you do not have to, though I do appreciate your work with the other seniors on the flowers. I think they make a big difference."

Siena's confusion must have registered on her face because Libby turned to explain the shorthand they all had with one another. "Aunt Emma sold bits and bobs last year in the mercantile space to get us started. And her senior living group planted all the flower baskets and the flowers in the town square."

"They are very pretty," Siena said.

"Thank you, dear," Aunt Emma replied. "Now Libby, what about the Dance Pavilion? That was another promise we made."

"Yes, so, to get you up to speed, Siena, our Dance Pavilion is historic. Back in the day, Brenda Lee, The Dorsey Brothers, Roy Orbison, and all of the big names performed in it. It was a roller-skating date night place when the Sandbar Sisters were tearing up the town," Libby said.

"Very cool."

"We just haven't gotten to it yet, but we will. It's on the way back. I just had to focus on the downtown first and then move out in circles, okay Aunt Emma?"

"So lazy, you're just sitting around doing nothing," Siena joked. These women had literally saved Irish Hills from the dust bin.

"Ladies, how are you all?"

A handsome man in a gorgeous suit that looked entirely out of place in the casual setting approached their table.

"Ugh, now I lost my appetite."

"J.J.," Libby scolded J.J.

"Sorry, sorry I forgot, he's not our mortal enemy anymore. It's hard to keep up."

"Hello," said the man to Siena, "I'm Stone Stirling, arch-nemesis of all things good and true in Irish Hills."

Siena was confused, but she shook the well-manicured hand that was offered.

"Stone is that developer who we bested to keep Irish Hills local and weird." J.J. had put a smile on her face. She did not like Stone Stirling. That was clear. But in Siena's estimation, he was handsome as heck for an older man and seemed nice.

"Yes, these days I'm just a lake homeowner, enjoying the work Libby has done. I've never been so happy to be wrong in my entire life. On that, I'm wondering if I could talk to you about an idea," Stone asked.

"I'm pretty booked."

"I'm at your service, whenever you have a free hour. Enjoy your lunches." Stone walked over to the counter and took a seat.

"Wow, he's handsome," Siena said.

"Wolf in billionaire's clothing, that's what I say," J.J. muttered.

"Oh, J.J., we won," Libby said. "He's just another summer resident these days. One who likes us—well, me—and he's better on our side than against it."

"She knows Bono. She gets uppity about things," J.J. said.

"Who knows, maybe he'll turn into a townie after all," Aunt Emma said.

"Please. Now let's get back to Siena's plans. I can't wait to be outfitted head to toe in Vivian Blackwood! Do they make short sizes? Ugh, vertically-challenged sizes," J.J. said with a nod to Aunt Emma.

"We can get you swathed in the chicest things we've got. No worries."

"It would be a step up from the t-shirt and jeans she wears every single day of the year." Aunt Emma said, and J.J. didn't disagree.

"I just don't want to get hair dye on the good stuff. It would be a shame to ruin couture."

"We're not couture."

"Well, you *are* fancy. Fancier than anything we've had around here since they opened Kohl's in Adrian."

Siena wasn't sure if J.J. was serious or joking.

"Yeah, that's my worry," Emma said.

"Worry?" Siena replied.

"Never mind, you were saying?"

They finished lunch while Siena explained her big plans. But all of a sudden, she was a little worried too.

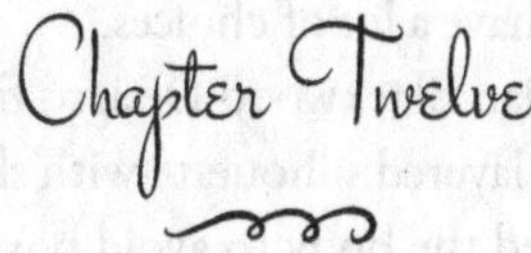

Chapter Twelve

Viv

"Hack." Viv looked at her sketch. The lines were clean. The jacket was sleek. There was nothing really wrong with the new idea she'd created for Vivian Blackwood Designs, but there was nothing right with it either.

She'd been in her room sketching and then on the little balcony, and now, she sat on the porch of the Two Lakes Grove and assessed the last four hours of work.

At least it wasn't a mass of black scribbling. Maybe that was progress.

But it wasn't going to change the world.

Vivian had changed the world, well, a little corner of it, once.

Her first line of clothing had turned career-wear on its ear.

Women in the workplace in the nineties and early two-thousands were dressed like men. There were structured blazers and matching pantsuits.

That slid into the Ally McBeal era. The popularity of the show with a lawyer in micro-mini skirts had women in the real world trying to copy the look. There was no happy medium. You either wore a "power suit," or you were yanking on a skirt that was riding up while you tried to give a presentation.

Women who wanted to be fashionable but professional, pretty but powerful, didn't have a lot of choices.

That's where Vivian Blackwood Designs filled the gap.

She had created a layered silhouette with skirts that came to the knee but also skimmed the body to avoid boxiness. She'd designed softer duster-style jackets to layer over the top. Vivian Blackwood Designs took off like a rocket for women who worked in banks, law firms, school administration, and even those breaking corporate glass ceilings. She was the go-to tastemaker.

She was in touch with the women of her generation. There were magazine interviews, and she'd even been featured on the breakfast shows in New York.

Viv was never blocked or stumped on what to design. She thought of Libby's lanky frame and her innate grace. She was guided by what made her feel pulled together in her own big meetings and presentations. And her pencil flew over her sketch book year after year. She layered new pieces in new colors, but her clothes were timeless. A woman could keep that skirt or jacket, or blouse for years and update it with the latest Vivian Blackwood piece or accessory. It wasn't fast fashion; it was the opposite.

But truth be told, sales had gotten softer. Even before her cancer, there were fewer department stores picking up the designs. Her clothes weren't a new idea anymore. Viv didn't have the sense that she knew what people wanted to wear to look professional. Had she gotten too old to do this? Had the industry and style passed her by?

Now, trying to freshen them up, after all she'd been through, felt like drawing with her opposite hand. The ease she once had was gone.

Maybe the need was gone too. A woman in her twenties

entering the workforce today didn't need or want the classic Vivian Blackwood look.

Today's workplace was casual, open to just about anything, and half the time, the big meeting was in a Zoom call, not a board room.

Viv took her pencil and scrawled a big "x" over the sketch that, just a moment ago, she'd considered okay.

"I agree. What a load of crap."

She didn't have to turn around to see who it was.

"Mr. Taggert, you're a fashion expert now?"

"Oh, for sure, and that looks like an outfit for my grandma."

"Thanks a lot."

Though he wasn't wrong, Viv didn't particularly feel like giving this brash near stranger the satisfaction of being right about her designs.

"I'm kidding. I have no idea about fashion. I wear what they pay me to wear."

"Excuse me?"

"You don't mind if I sit here, do you?"

"The porch is for all the guests; you can sit where you please." Viv was irritated by this man, even though he seemed to be trying to make friends.

"I appreciate it."

"So, you wear what they pay you to wear? Are you some sort of model?"

"Ha," Tag laughed.

It was contagious, and Viv smiled, despite the fact she was half worried he was making fun of her.

"I'm sorry, it's just in my world. We pay models to wear stuff."

"I'm no model. I'm a racecar driver. All this is courtesy of my line of work." He pointed to the bum leg and the cuts that were looking less angry.

"Oh, wow, sorry about that."

"Nah, unless you were driving the number nine car at the

Flamekeepers Casino 400 and got on my bumper over at Michigan International Speedway."

"I was not."

"In terms of fashion, if it says Red Bull on the hat or Penzoil on the jacket and they paid for the spot, I wear it."

"Oh, okay, I see. Well, right now, I'm not really a fashion expert, either. I used to be, but pfft." Viv made another scribble on the design.

"You're on the mend too, I hear."

Viv stiffened up a bit. What did this guy know about her cancer battle?

"Relax, I just accidentally overheard your friend Goldie clucking over you and your need to rest and heal and blah blah blah. You know, all the get-well crap I've been hearing lately, too."

Viv did relax a little. It would be hard not to hear Goldie or Siena, or J.J., fussing over her every time they visited in the last few days. They wanted to take care of her, and she was grateful.

"I think my diagnosis has turned into my entire personality."

"What now?" He leaned his right side to her.

"Oh, uh, my cancer has turned into my entire personality." She changed the diagnosis to cancer on purpose. She may as well answer the question since Taggert seemed willing to ask her whatever came to mind.

"Oh, I get ya. If I have to hear one more thing about taking it easy, I'm going to blow a gasket."

Viv laughed. She was sick of being the sick one, she realized.

"You know, as a taste maker, perhaps you can do me a favor?"

"How's that?"

"I just bought a new place up the road, and I'd love to get a woman's perspective on what needs to be fixed up. Especially a fashionable woman."

"I don't know. I'm supposed to be doing this sketch and—"

"—And resting, yes, you're supposed to be resting. I wonder if you might transfer your old self to a rocker right over there. We could get you a blanket over your knees. Put a record on an old Victrola for you."

"You're pretty bold for someone who's looking like he couldn't outrun a recent cancer patient who's lost her will to live."

Viv didn't know what had come over her. Tag was teasing her, pushing her even, and she'd blurted out something that would have caused an uproar among her friends and family. They'd have called the support group and circled wagons. They'd have bent over backward to reassure her. They wanted to fix her. Understandable. But impossible.

The comment hung in the air. Maybe it was also a bridge too far for this smart-mouthed near stranger.

"Well, if you're going out, you're going out swinging."

Viv couldn't stop a smile from spreading across her face. "I think you might be a bad influence."

"Think it? I know it. Now, what do you say? I'm a professional driver. You'll be safe as can be."

"Says the man who just busted up his car and face at what, 100 miles per hour?"

"Details."

She decided to do it. Why not? Viv wasn't getting any work done with her sketch, and at least Larson Taggert got her dark sense of humor. "Alright, I'll take a look with my artistic eye to see if you got hosed on a white elephant property."

"Much obliged. I'll figure out a way to pay you back. Model something for free."

She laughed at the suggestion.

The two of them made their way to Tag's car, and as she'd expected, it was a convertible. Why did she know this was going to be the case?

Well, her hair couldn't be any jankier after the last few months. She may as well drive with the top down.

"What is this?"

"This is a vintage 1966 Ford Mustang Convertible. It's like my child. So, if you don't think she's pretty, do not say so where I can hear, ha, made a joke." He pointed to his scratched-up face and ear.

Viv was getting the idea that the injury to his leg and face wasn't all he'd suffered.

"Oh, she's pretty alright."

"I heard that at least!"

Rolling through the countryside wasn't going to make her hair any worse. What she did not expect was the peeling out of the fast turns and the hooting and hollering accompanying this little country drive.

"Where did you say this property was?"

"Other side of the lake, I just needed to drive a little bit." He had circled Manitou Lake twice before taking the smaller inlet roads to the lake front property.

When they arrived at the property, the house, the yard, something about it felt familiar to her. But then again, she had traveled a lot of these paths back in the day on her bike. She probably would start to recognize a lot if she got out of the hotel a bit.

The place was shabby and overgrown, and it was clear that it had seen better days.

"This is it? You must be kind of a sucky race car driver?"

It was a two-story cottage that maybe was cute back in 1950-something, but it looked pieced together, added on, and essentially neglected.

"Hey, I was at the top of my game before Evans Wallace Turk and I tangled chrome, lady. You clearly don't know how famous I am in certain circles."

"Ah, sure."

"Now, normally, I'd come around and open the door for you, like a gentleman, but if I do that, it could be, oh, several hours before we successfully get out of the vehicle."

"Don't worry about it. It's not like we're going to prom."

Viv got out and was around to help Tag before he was out of his side. Navigating with a broken leg, a brace, and crutches did slow a person down. It was actually refreshing not to be the one most in need of help. Viv grabbed the crutches out of the back seat and held them as Tag navigated to vertical.

"I hate these things so much. But thank you. I mean, if my mother saw a woman helping me out of the car, she'd roll over in her grave."

"So, when did you buy this place?"

"Last week, fire sale—literally, there was a fire in the garage over there. Luckily, it's not attached, and honestly, I can build my own outbuilding now, the way I want."

Viv looked at the charred heap that he'd indicated used to be the garage.

They made their way to the house, and he unlocked to door and ushered her in.

It was, as advertised, a time capsule of kitsch. The appliances were a mishmash of avocado and harvest gold. The carpet was an orange shag. The walls were Brady Bunch paneling; damaged Brady Bunch paneling, to be exact.

But it was big, a huge great room and sliders that looked out to the back, to the lake.

"I like the décor. I think I'll just leave that. What do you think?"

"You're nuts. You need to rip out the carpet, the walls. I mean, I can't even image the bathrooms. Pink, I'm going to guess."

"Yeah, kidding. I know it needs major work. I will say the inspector said the foundation is good. Plumbing and electrical. Not so much."

Viv walked around the place.

"Did you pay extra for the furnishings?"

"Yeah, it was an estate sale. Poor old dude passed on a few years ago, but the kids were fighting and decided to sell and split the proceeds. I've got to clear it all out. But hey, it'll be part of the rehab."

Viv scanned the rooms. Three bedrooms, a huge rec room off

the living/kitchen area, and a basement walk-out below made her think he had something here. It was a great location too.

"Oh, is that what I think it is?"

Viv looked out to the lake frontage. There was a big old tree with a branch that stretched out over the lake. It sat next to a sandy beach that needed raking. But could it be?

She walked to the back screen and, with a bit of struggle, opened it to the outside.

"Go at your own pace. I'll keep up." She turned to see if Tag was kidding, but he didn't appear to be.

"I think I know this place." She walked out to the backyard and toward the big tree.

She broke into a little run.

It couldn't be, really?

And there it was! A tattered but thick rope dangled from the branch of the tree.

She looked out over the water and remembered again. This was the place! The Ewald place. She'd taken a leap here into the water and got shot at.

She was a kid here. She hadn't been here since she'd swum for her life out of here, decades ago.

"Tag. I need to get up there."

"What?"

"I'm serious. I need to get up there." She pointed to the rope and the little disc they'd used to balance on.

"Oh great, your friend Goldie's going to think I slipped you some drugs, and you've started to hallucinate."

"Tag, I'm either going up there on my own, or you can help me."

"You're nuts."

"Maybe."

"I kind of like it."

Between the two of them, they got the rope free.

Tag grabbed it and pulled on it. "It feels pretty secure."

"Thanks, okay, so. You're going to push me."

"I figured. Are you sure about this? I mean, your friends and family seem to think you're already a cracked eggshell. And my push could have me crashing down. Balance ain't the strong suit right now, you get it?"

"I'm sure about this, and you'll be fine. Really. I trust you." She trusted him? What was she saying? Viv had decided to throw caution to the wind all of a sudden. She was compelled by something she didn't quite understand but didn't feel like stopping to analyze.

Viv knew it was her recent memory of this very moment. Why had that memory come to her? After all these years? Why had she wound up right here?

Nothing in the last year had been fun, nothing had been alive, nothing had been hopeful. She'd lived in a scared state. She'd worried about food, rest, stitches, energy, treatments, positive thinking, negative thinking, her financial affairs, her living will, her business, and just everything. And nothing. More than half the time, her mind would go blank, she'd lose her train of thought, or she couldn't concentrate.

Seeing that rope put one thing on her mind. No amount of logic or warning was going to divert her.

"Okay, just know, I can drag you back in, but it will take a second to get my brace off before I can jump in if you start drowning."

"I'm not doing a cliff dive in Mexico, for goodness' sake. It's a rope in Irish Hills. Besides, I've done it before. I'm not going to drown. You won't even get a splash on you."

"Okay."

Viv took off her shoes. And grabbed the rope. Her grip was tight. She looked out into the water. It was the same, exactly the same. She knew it was deep enough if she let go when the rope arched.

"You don't really push; you pull back on the rope and then let it rip." Tag grabbed the top of the rope above her head as she issued her directive. They were nose to nose.

"You're a whack job, you realize it, right?"

"Ha, yeah, takes one to know one." Viv had lost all reason, she'd supposed, at this minute.

"Okay, don't forget to let go or—"

"I'll slam back into the tree. Oh, trust me, I know."

They locked eyes. Viv recognized something in Tag, and he in her. They'd both recently faced a death sentence, or nearly so. Maybe that was it. And maybe seeing him not give a tinker's damn about being gentle with himself was a good prompting for her. She wasn't as easy to break as she thought. Who knew? What she did know was what it was like to sail through the air right here.

"Ready?"

"Yep. Let it rip."

Viv squeezed the rope with her arms, and she tightened her legs around it. She realized there would be no chance of her holding on too long. She'd barely cleared the shore. But she was going to do it.

Tag leaned on his good leg. She felt a little bad, he'd probably lose his balance executing this maneuver. But he didn't seem to mind.

Tag pulled the rope back and held it for a second, close to his side, and then he let go. She zipped through the air up, over the lakeshore, and when the water was below her, she let go. She squealed.

She was maybe six or eight feet up. The lake came at her fast, and she splashed in. The cold water woke her up, it almost hurt, but it didn't kill her. No, it did not!

She kicked her legs. They were stiff, and her body wasn't used to any of this dramatic activity. But it did remember. She remembered. She kicked again and broke the surface. She took a breath. She rolled onto her back and floated for a second. Viv looked up at the sky.

It was clear blue. She was still, for a second, in the water.

"You, okay?" Tag had inched down to the sandy beach on his backside.

"Leave your brace on. I'm perfect. No worries." He didn't need to come in and rescue her. No one did.

She could jump into the deep water and swim back out.

She paddled toward the shore, and when it was shallow enough, she stood up and walked back out.

"How was that?"

"Cold."

"You got a lot of airtime there, lady." He offered his one free hand, but she didn't need it. She found her own balance.

"Yes." She hadn't thought about the aftermath: no towel, no change of clothes. Her teeth started to chatter a little. She was dripping wet, and her clothes were now heavy. It was the first few days of June, still, spring and not yet warm enough to be standing around in wet clothes. She wrung out her skirt.

"Uh, I think we have towels in the house. Let's go check. You aren't getting in my baby all soggy."

"I didn't really think too far in advance here." She laughed at the impulsive decision she'd made. Siena would have stopped her. Bret would have tried to talk her out of it. She knew their caution was all about worry for her, but still.

"The closet in there has stuff that needs clearing out. Maybe a towel, here—yes!" Tag had found her a towel. She felt bad dripping all over his house, but then again, the place needed to be gutted.

Viv walked into a closet that was stuffed with clothes. Well, beggars can't be choosers. She'd switch out of her wet clothes for the ride back to the hotel. The house might be a mess, but his car was nice. She didn't really want to drip all over the leather seats.

After drying off, Viv balled her wet clothes into the old towel. She stood naked in the closet. There were t-shirts, polyester shorts, and a few buttoned blouses, and then something bright orange caught her eye. It was on a hanger but nearly touched the floor.

Viv took the garment off the rack and admired it. It was diaphanous silk. There was a V-neck, two giant arm holes, and slits on the sides.

"What in the Mrs. Roper?"

She slid it off the hangar and put it to her nose. It smelled of Shalimar. Wow. Blast from the past on that.

"At least it's not moldy," Viv said to herself as she gathered the fabric and popped her head through. She easily found the arm holes, and voila, she was in the muumuu. Or was it a kaftan? She'd have to research that little detail. Either way, she was comfortable, dry, and feeling gloriously diva-like.

She never acted the diva, but she'd also never worn such a glorious garment.

Viv picked up the rolled-up towel with the wet clothes nestled inside and rejoined Tag in the kitchen.

"So, this yellow and green appliance thing isn't coming back? I could keep them and be hip?"

"No, they're out."

"Speaking of hip, you look groovy."

"Thank you. And thank you for the help taking the plunge."

"My pleasure. As soon as I can use this leg, I'm going to have you return the favor."

"Deal. Now take a few pics of your space. I'll think about some fixes for you. The least I could do."

"You don't owe me anything."

"Oh, yes, I do. I'm keeping this." With that, Viv walked confidently out of the old cottage. And boldly, a new idea blossomed in her heart as silky orange fabric billowed around her.

Chapter Thirteen

Siena

"Yep, got 'em. I talked to Molly. She's creating all of them right now. Yep. Sure. See you for dinner? Great. Get some rest."

Siena got off the call with her mother and should have been reassured. But she wasn't. The truth was she'd been struggling to make the balance sheets balance for two years, even before her mother's cancer. What she'd got from her mom didn't seem to be the answer. Then again...

It's not that the designs weren't lovely. It's just that they were similar to the previous few years. That was the Vivian Blackwood look. That's what their customers wanted. The last few years had been tough on all kinds of businesses. Siena knew they'd bounce back; she was going to be sure of it. Molly, their seamstress, was working on putting a few pieces together to display in the store. It would be okay.

The store was almost ready.

Aunt Libby was handling making sure everyone in the tri-state area was headed to Irish Hills for the Sunshine Days, the summer kick-off in the region.

There was even a magazine writer from Detroit coming to do a feature on their flagship shop. That's right, flagship. Siena was thinking positively.

What she didn't have were enough décor pieces to stage the store, to make it feel more welcoming and less like a big room with hangars and mirrors. She wanted minimalism, but what she had right now was cold and boring.

She needed to find a few things to make the place feel warmer and to keep the customers in the store while they browsed.

Siena was headed on an adventure to find some things to warm up the space. This was good. This was fine-tuning. She would tweak the place and get the feel they needed. She knew she'd make the deadline for the opening. She just had to stay positive.

She also wasn't letting this type of detail get through to her mom. She was the one who'd insisted on coming here, on the store, and on this course for their lives. It was up to Siena to let her mom do what she had to do to continue to get better. Despite her worries about sales and the new line, her mother had been different in the last few days. She seemed almost like her old self. Siena reminded herself that was the whole point.

She locked up the store and headed to the Tecumseh Trade Center and Flea Market. The motto was, "If someone here doesn't have it or can't get it, no one makes it."

She'd heard about it from a few residents. It was open on weekends and claimed to have a huge collection of vendors. Hopefully, it was big enough to offer a good selection for her to choose from. It was about a forty-five-minute drive to some place between Tecumseh and a town called Clinton. She'd never been to either. Plus, she didn't have a big enough vehicle if she found something she needed to haul. Siena and her mother had driven the Volvo here, and it barely fit their luggage.

But Aunt Libby had come to the rescue again and hooked her

up with Cole Brady. He worked with his dad, Keith Brady, at the marina. He had a pickup truck and time on his hands today.

Siena was ready to go when Cole Brady's truck pulled up. She locked the front door and came out to discover that Cole Brady had rushed around to the passenger door.

"Hi, I'm Cole." Siena rarely had to look up to anyone. She did have to look up to meet the eyes of Cole Brady. His blue eyes were framed with dark eye lashes, gorgeous. But that was about the only soft-looking thing about his face. He had a tough stubble edging his strong jaw. She couldn't help but notice the broad shoulders and corded forearms. Get a grip, Siena. This is just a guy doing a favor for his dad's girlfriend to help you haul a big flea market find. She tried not to act like a dorky schoolgirl.

Siena snapped out of her gawking and responded. "I'm Siena."

"I cleaned out the truck as best as I could, but it's best not to open the glove box and do me a favor and ignore the taco smell. I had that for lunch yesterday while driving, and well, it's just not pretty."

"I'll crack a window. Besides, you're doing me a favor."

Cole opened the passenger door, and Siena climbed in. It was an old truck, it looked tidy enough, but as Cole sat in the driver's seat, she put her finger on it.

"Nachos Supreme?"

"Yes, good nose. I love 'em."

"I haven't seen a fast-food place in Irish Hills."

"We're going to the Tecumseh, right? They've got fast food. Or we can head over to Brooklyn. After we can go to Poppa's Place, they've got a great ham and cheese."

"Sounds good!"

Siena hadn't spent much time with anyone her age other than enjoying Lila's company when she brought lunch. Other than that, it had been all old aunts and doctors for over a year.

"You're from Irish Hills?"

"Well, we moved here when I was a teenager. Before that, all over the place with my dad's deployments. But I'd say it's my hometown more than any other place."

"I haven't explored much. I've been knee-deep in getting the store ready."

"Are you a designer like your mom?"

"Yes and no. She is a clothing designer; her degree is in fashion design. My degree is in merchandising to help the family business. That's what this project is all about. Expanding Mom's business."

"Cool."

"You work at your dad's marina?"

"That I do. He fixes the boats, I schedule the dock space, help winterize, and sometimes gas 'em up. Whatever we need to do. We had been keeping up with only two of us, but it's getting busier. Need more hands-on deck."

"Oh, I'm so appreciative that you had time for this."

"Are you kidding? I was dying to meet you. Now I have a legit reason."

Siena blushed and changed the subject. "Well, thank you anyway."

They drove through country roads, painted barns dotted the landscape, and Siena wondered again about what she'd planned for the store. She saw clearly that she needed to bring more of what was special about the area into the boutique, not just her mother's clothing designs but her mother's designs against a backdrop of the Irish Hills.

Cole wasn't overly chatty, nor did he interrupt her train of thought. But the periods of silence were comfortable, not awkward. She asked him about the different places he lived and his family. She found out his mom passed a few years back, cancer.

"We all took on a lot of the things she used to do, but we couldn't quite do it was well as she did." He was being self-effacing.

"Yeah, my mom is in recovery. That's why I'm doing all the stuff for the store. I just want it to be easy for her."

"Sure."

She hadn't expected to meet someone who knew exactly what she was going through with her mom, but there he was, right next to her behind the wheel. Giving up a Friday to do her a favor. It was pretty darn sweet.

Cole slowed down and swooped his hand across the dashboard as if to present the Tecumseh Trade Center like he was Vanna White.

"You've been here before?"

"Yes, my mother insisted, back when we bought the marina. She has vintage Miller High Life signs and an old Coca-Cola cooler. It's all pretty cool, that stuff."

"I'm betting you're glad she did."

"I learned never to say no to a woman who wants to go antiquing, from the best of 'em."

"I owe her a debt of thanks."

"Just so you think, I'm not a saint, I also had a bad date here, and that girl and I did not work out." Siena was weirdly glad to hear that.

"Well, this isn't a date. It's a mission."

"Roger that." Cole gave her a salute, and they set off into the wilds of the flea market.

There were booths outside, but also two massive red barns with rows and rows of vendors.

They strolled the booths. Siena spotted three tables with glass tops that were perfect for displaying scarves and accessories, and she could probably use one in the breakroom.

"Oh, these are perfect. Can we load these?"

Cole easily hoisted the things she'd found onto his shoulders and transported them to the truck. She also discovered a vendor with the coolest vases she'd ever seen. Maybe she could use those on a few shelves, fill them with flowers, and warm up the vibe in the store.

She bought half a dozen, and those made it to the truck too.

"I'm thinking you need to buy something soft to be sure this stuff doesn't break," Cole said as he puzzled over how to secure her growing pile of treasures.

"Yes, thanks. It looks like textiles are in that far row."

Cole dutifully followed her as she explored. Siena wound up with a few table runners but then found a booth with unique knitted throw blankets.

"I need these." She blurted it out but then realized she didn't know what she needed them for. She was supposed to be finding pieces to decorate the space. They didn't need blankets. Unless...

After another two hours of shopping and careful rearranging, Siena wound up with two chairs that she planned to paint and a chest of drawers to redo. She'd put the blankets on the chairs, and the chest of drawers could hold Vivian Blackwood camisoles and other basics. The blankets, well, there was no reason to have a dozen. But Siena bought the entire lot on display.

She also found an artist that had lovely botanical watercolors for sale.

"These would be perfect against the brick walls with those gold frames we saw over there."

Cole and Siena made trip after trip.

Finally, Cole had reached the limit. Rather, his truck did. They couldn't fit a single added item in the back.

"If you need more, we may have to drop off this stuff and come back," Cole said. He climbed down from the truck after assuring her everything was a secure as it could be.

"I think we're good. Oh, wait, can we go to that last booth over there? I just want to look at the prints they're selling."

Cole looked at Siena and narrowed his eyes, then he perused the state of the pickup. "Okay, I mean, if they're narrow, we could slide them right here."

"Yes!"

Cole laughed at her enthusiasm, but he was game to help.

Maybe she'd help expunge any bad flea market memories with this trip.

Cole and Siena made one more trek across the barn.

"You're confident."

"What?"

"You seem to know exactly what pieces you want, and boom, you decide."

"Well, I have a vision for what the store could look like. I want shoppers to come and feel peaceful, welcomed, but also envious!"

"What?"

"They need to want the vibe we create for their own lives. That's the key."

"I get it. I mean, I don't get it, but I get it. And believe me, it's nice to see the decisiveness. I had no idea all this went into selling women's outfits."

It probably didn't, but this was the first time she'd set up a boutique. She could only go by her instincts.

"I take it your date was not decisive the last time you were here."

"No, nice enough, girl, but honestly, we stood in each booth forever. She'd load up stuff, and put it back, and load it and put it back. I apologized to vendor after vendor for the amount of time she took and didn't buy. That part was rude, in my estimation."

"Ah, well, that's not my issue. I know what I know and like what I like."

"Me too," Cole said.

All of a sudden, Siena realized they might not be talking about shopping. She blushed but decided to soldier on. She liked Cole, and he was the first dateable male she had spent any time with in almost a year. She took a risk. "Well, good, because I think we're going to go on a date."

Cole smiled.

Man, he had a nice smile.

"I like your thinking," he replied, "but can it be other than a flea market?"

"Deal, how about lunch? I hear there's a great place in Brooklyn. It's on me."

"Nice. Now let's see if those wall hangings fit your vision."

They walked to the booth Siena wanted to check, and after a little haggling, the prints were in the truck. This was twice the number she needed, but like she told Cole, she knew what she liked.

And she liked the flea market and her driver a whole heck of a lot.

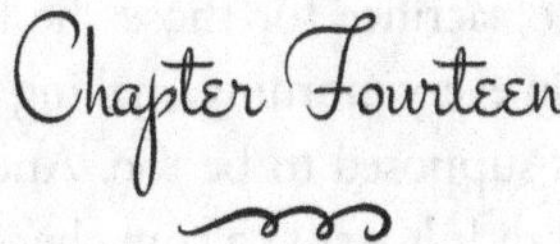

Chapter Fourteen

Viv

Viv had turned in her designs to Siena.

Completing that task, even though it hadn't been all that successful, freed her up to do what she really wanted to do.

The borrowed muumuu had sparked something in her. But she needed an accomplice if she wanted to run with this new inspiration.

To her delight, Tag was her willing high-speed chauffeur. He happily drover her through the country roads into Adrian so she could get the raw materials to create what was in her head.

While Siena was in and out, busy setting up the store, she was sure that Viv was sleeping, paddling, boating, and sunning. But in reality, she was in a frenzy of her own, drawing and sewing.

Goldie also facilitated her need for fabrics and notions.

"I thought you were supposed to be sleeping," Goldie said as they shared coffee on the porch. Goldie herself was working a lot, too, on calls with her new TV series project. But the two women checked in each morning, and Goldie was determined to be sure Viv had anything her heart desired.

This was her movie star friend. The world saw Goldie as a Hollywood Diva, but Viv saw Goldie as she truly was: giving, loving, and willing to sacrifice for those she loved. That was the Goldie that checked in every morning, making sure Viv was okay.

"I thought I was supposed to be too. And to be honest with you, I love you, but I didn't want to come here. I just didn't know what I wanted."

"It's okay. You've been through the wringer. Siena is young. She's gung-ho about all of the things. We know better."

"But I'm glad we're here. I do feel energized. Maybe the lake air, that first huge nap day, who knows, but I'm feeling better."

"Maybe it's Tag?"

"Ha, what are you saying?"

"I'm saying that hunk of a racecar driver would get my motor running too."

"Stop, we're friends. My sexy days are over."

"I wouldn't be so sure."

"I will say, taking me to the fabric store in Adrian, driving me to get that sewing machine for my room, that's been amazing. And he seems to appreciate the excuse to drive."

"You know, his crash was terrible. Horrifying, really. We saw it live because Joe dragged me to the race. They're old friends. Anyway, you're not the only one on the mend."

"I think that's actually helped us bond. We're both missing a few parts."

"Well, I'm just glad you're finding some happy."

"I am, and your open door and open heart are a huge reason why."

"Shh, don't tell. I'm a cutthroat producer now."

"It's our little secret."

"The season is going to be crazy around here, good crazy but crazy. You up for the festivities Libby has planned?"

"I'm looking forward to it. I haven't been to Nora House since that tornado. I can hardly believe we're all back here."

"Okay, I've got a few things to do, and then I'm going to drive us over on my new toy. He's invited Tag, is that cool with you?"

Viv didn't want to be paired up with Tag like they were a couple, but she also enjoyed his company.

"It's fine. What can I bring, did Libby say?"

"I'm handling it, I've got wine, and Hope's doing a ton of food. Just bring your beautiful self."

Viv sighed. She knew she should get a gift or wine or something for her first visit to Nora House since they'd been to Irish Hills. It was polite. It was what she should do.

"You are all treating me like a baby. I know how to be a good guest."

Goldie reached out and grabbed her hand.

"I know you do. But you're not a guest. None of us are. This is home. You'll see. Now, be ready at noon. I'll honk when we're ready to go."

"Thank you, love."

Viv went up to her room. She had overtaken a corner with the little sewing machine and bits and bobs she'd collected. In the closet hung about a dozen of her creations. She'd made one a day since her plunder at Tag's.

Kaftans or tunics or muumuus, whatever you wanted to call them, were what had sparked her creative passion. It was unexpected, and she was supposed to be creating more career wear. But she just couldn't. Business-like, neutral, and in control—she didn't feel any of those things right now.

What she wanted was something flowing, comfortable, regal even. She was maybe in her Mrs. Roper phase. Did all women get a Mrs. Roper phase? Maybe it would pass. But the moment she put that cover-up on in Tag's place, she was hot to buy more.

Except she didn't see any that she really loved. She searched online, retail stores, eBay, and Poshmark; nothing was right.

And just like that, she started sketching what she wanted. Her pencil flew over the paper, and then she switched from her black pencil to her colored pencils.

The sketches were vibrant and flowing, and they kept coming. She had to bring them into the world. Tag had helped her get the materials and then replenish them when she ran out. Viv just kept going.

All the while, Siena thought she was napping or at the least working on a new line for Vivian Blackwood, but instead, it was these kaftans.

She had silk, satin, cotton, linen, and chiffon.

She'd experimented with different cuts and necklines. Each one was a little different. But she was starting to get a feel for three styles that she liked the best. That said, it wasn't cookie-cutter. She liked doing each by hand. She liked detailing them and embellishing them with trim that made each piece its own creation. Today, for their trip to Nora House and their day on the boat, she would debut her favorite.

The garment was lavender with gold detailing. It was silk, and she had gold sandals to pair with it.

She lifted it over her head. There was a little twinge when she made the motion, but the doctor had told her things would get more comfortable. The flowy kaftan eliminated her worrying about what to wear or how to be, it was light, feminine, and beautiful, and she was starting to see Elizabeth Taylor.

Viv stepped in front of the mirror. Viv didn't cringe. For the first time in a long while, she felt pleased with what she saw. J.J. had given her an adorable hairstyle. Her hair was full on the top, with choppy layers all around. There was some shape to it. It moved when she did. It had life. It was chic but, dare she say it, sexy!

She was even inspired to put on a little makeup. Viv had dark circles these days, but she was also good at covering them. She dabbed on some concealer, a little mascara, and some blush. A swipe of lip gloss. She was ready.

Viv smiled at her reflection. Her heart felt light. She felt beautiful. When was the last time she felt that? She honestly didn't know.

She jumped a foot or so in the air when she heard the honk coming from the waterside, not the front entrance of the hotel.

Viv looked outside to the water, and there was Goldie about to lay on the horn again to the most ostentation pontoon boat she'd ever seen.

Viv watched Joe tie it to the dock and Tag walk out to the thing. She had a little worry, could Tag get onboard without a helping hand? But she watched as he lifted his bum leg and hopped on with his good leg. He didn't let his rehab stop him. He'd shed the crutches of late and had a boot that he could more easily navigate.

Viv grabbed her bag and decided it was a good attitude to have. She wasn't going to let the last few months ruin the next few weeks. Her days may be numbered, but if they were, they were going to be fun days.

She went outside to the boat.

"What in the name of all that is good and holy is this thing?"

"I'm calling her *The Cleopatra*. She's our chariot to Nora House."

"Permission to come aboard?"

"Granted."

Joe and Tag both offered Viv a hand to climb on. She took both because if this was a Queen of the Nile kind of deal, why not?

"Now, be careful. You need to ease out. This isn't for peeling out." Joe told Goldie, who waved him off like he was a gnat.

"I've got the hang of it now."

"She nearly took the dock out over at Keith's when we picked it up," Joe told Viv under his breath.

Keith owned Steve's Marina now, and she could envision the scene.

"You've gone from limos and Ubers to driving your own pontoon boat, wow."

"Oh, I used to do this? Remember?"

"I do."

"I better hang on to something. I sense she's a speed demon." Tag sat next to Viv on the cushioned seats under the canopy of the wide porch-like boat. Viv had never seen a pontoon boat this luxe.

"Takes one to know one," said Viv.

The Cleopatra pontoon boat gleamed black and gold in the sun. Speakers embedded into the seats played The Chicks. Three shiny pontoons held the vessel on top of the water, and Viv did wonder how Goldie was going to avoid hitting things with it. The boat was enormous. The floor looked like real wood, for goodness' sake. Everywhere Viv looked, there was a cup holder. Or something glinting in the sun.

Joe opened a door to reveal a beverage fridge.

"Can I offer you some wine? White? Red?"

"Uh, Boone's Farm, maybe. Some Country Kwencher?"

"Ha! You're not quite as classy as you put out," Tag said.

"What, white wine seems appropriate to the day. Kwencher is a white." Viv shrugged. She had no idea what was actually appropriate for this floating palace.

"Classy, this girl hurled her guts out for the entire night when we were, what, seventeen, after Keith got us Bellagio?"

"Shh, do not tell Siena these awful lies," Viv said. That experience cured her of binge drinking.

"We did have some fun," Goldie said.

"We were lucky, the trouble we narrowly avoided in those days." The memory of those summer nights warmed Viv.

Joe handed her a glass of white, decidedly a few steps up from Boone's Farm.

"So, international superstar Goldie Hayes used to tool

around the lake, raising hell?" Joe asked, and you could see while he liked teasing Goldie, he also just liked Goldie. He was not in awe of the star but charmed by the person. Goldie deserved that, finally.

"Oh, we all did. Libby had a pontoon back then, but she also had a little fishing boat that we all crammed into most of the time," Viv said.

"I only ran it aground once. I think that's pretty good."

"Oh, man," Joe said and shook his head.

"She ran it aground once and also got it stuck in the sandbar for half a day once."

"Pfft." Goldie waved off the old stories.

The air was warm if you were still, but gliding over the lake with the wind, Viv felt a little chill all of a sudden.

"Here, slide out from the canopy. The sun will warm you up." Tag said Viv appreciated his thoughtfulness.

She had trouble getting warm enough lately. She slid out of the shade and let the sun hit her.

How many times had she glided over these waters?

More times than she could count.

The Cleopatra arrived at Nora House like the famed Egyptian Queen touring the Nile. Except there was a horn honk that scared the living daylights out of an unsuspecting family of mallard ducks.

"Fisherman are going to love you," Joe said.

Viv took in the house. It was the same. The tornado in '89 took out a tree, and the barn looked redone, but essentially the old girl was the same. It comforted Viv, as an old girl herself, to see the stately beauty of Nora House. It had survived the brutal cyclone that had gutted so much of Irish Hills.

Libby had her hands on her hips on the dock. She was shaking her head as *The Cleopatra* slid into port. She was more cruise ship than a pontoon in her maneuverability.

"It's like the *Titanic*, for crying out loud. It makes my poor thing look like crap." Libby's pontoon boat looked to be the very same one they'd grown up on.

The rest of the Sandbar Sisters were waiting on the beach of Nora House. The new boat got the same reaction from them as she did Viv.

"Wow, you know, you could do dinner cruises on this thing," said Hope.

"I suppose maybe the guests would like that."

"No way, I want this available for my personal use whenever I want it," J.J. said as her husband Dean helped ensure Goldie's captaining didn't take out the entire dock. They grabbed lines and adjusted bumpers.

"My son tells me you're all stretched to the max between the restaurant and the inn."

It was Keith Brady. Viv gasped a little, taking in the face of another old friend. The same, but better in some ways, weathered a little more over the decades.

With *The Cleopatra* safely docked, Tag hopped out, and Keith was there with a hand for him and then for Viv.

"I can't believe it, Viv. You're a sight for sore eyes." Keith pulled her into a hug.

He was the big brother she never had, the one they all never had. Well, except Libby. She remembered their breakup like it had happened to her. Other girls had *General Hospital*, the Sandbar Sisters had the romance of Keith and Libby, and the seemingly worldly way with men that Hope had. For Viv, those two were her teachers.

"One of the first things I remembered when I got into town was our swinging adventure back in the day."

"Swinging?" Joe said, and he looked shocked.

"Ha, no, Keith and I back on the day we both went flying into the lake on this really cool rope swing, just as the owner of the property we were trespassing on came back and started shooting!"

"Oh, yeah, Ewald started shooting his B.B. gun." J.J. remembered too.

"Yeah, and we had to swim for our lives," Keith recalled. He walked with Viv, an arm around her. She put her head on his shoulder. Why hadn't she kept in touch with all these people? There was a pang of regret at the time lost. And the lives they'd all lived that she hadn't the first clue about.

They all made their way to the expansive back porch of Nora House. Everyone chimed in with tidbits of memory from that day.

"Ewald called my Aunt Emma and explained how lucky we were that he didn't call the cops."

"Oooh, what did she say?" Goldie asked.

"Something about he could kiss her backside. She wasn't a fan of threats or anyone bossing her around. Still isn't," Libby said.

Libby and Hope disappeared inside and re-emerged with beverages.

"The food is all laid out in the kitchen, and Keith has agreed to be my sous chef when anyone's ready for burgers," Hope said, coming over to hug Viv. "Okay, where did you get this kaftan? I need one."

"Ah, I made it. My career wear wasn't cutting it for hanging out at the lake, so I made this. I have decided to live in it for the summer."

"Darn, I was hoping you'd say Amazon. I'd have bought ten," Hope said.

Viv watched how her old friends had fallen into an easy rhythm with one another. Tag and Joe were new to the bunch, and so was she, really. But they felt welcomed and at ease. That was Libby; she'd brought them all here, one way or another, and she'd made them feel like a unit. She was a connector of people. That was a gift Viv didn't have.

Viv couldn't get over the gray stubble on Keith and remembered teasing him about his inability to grow a mustache back in the day.

Viv learned that Dean, J.J.'s husband, was beginning to do renovations on the buildings across the street from Hope's restaurant and the boutique.

"I'm not sure who I'm going to target for those spots—well, except I insist J.J. open a salon," Libby said.

"Please, Shelly at HairDo or Dye Beauty Parlor would have a heart attack if I left or poached her clients."

"She's close to retirement, and we can bring her with you," Libby said. Though she said she didn't have a plan, she clearly did.

"You know we need a bakery. That's what I vote for in that new space," J.J. said, deflecting Libby from talk of opening her own salon.

"I second that, or ooh, a bookstore, which would be a good one for you, Goldie," Hope said.

"You're already roping me in for rehabbing the dance pavilion as a theater, so I'm out on the bookstore idea. Besides, you know I'm gone half the year. A bookstore should be open year-round, right? Especially at the holidays," Goldie said.

Viv watched Goldie put a sandwich in her mouth. A sandwich with actual bread! She *had* changed since she had come back to Irish Hills.

"Okay, okay, enough shop talk. I heard your Cole, and your Siena are dating. I'd like the complete scoop, please," J.J. said.

"What? Wait, I had no idea," Viv replied. Normally Siena told her everything. This was news to her.

"Well, I'm not sure about dating. Braylon sent Cole to your store with a truck and his ability to lift heavy things. They seem to hit it off, but dating? I have not gotten official confirmation on this intel," Keith said.

"Ahem, I've served them dinner twice now. It looked like a date, quacked like a date, so it's a date," Hope added.

"Wow, okay, I've been trying to stay out of her way, letting her take the lead on the project, and instead, she's dating," Viv said.

"Ha, well, they're under fifty. They can do more than one

thing at a time. I'm unable to these days. I used to tease my mom for that, and now, oh my gosh, if I don't get a ten-minute catnap in the afternoon, forget it. I'm a zombie." J.J. said. Though it was hard to believe J.J. had anything but unlimited energy.

The conversation turned on its head to all manner of annoying things that happen in your fifties. Viv laughed as her girlfriends recounted the horrors of hot flashes, and Hope vowed never to exfoliate anything again.

"It's a full-time job. I do not have time," she said.

Though he wasn't in attendance, Viv heard Hope had a love interest these days as well. While Hope claimed not to have time for exfoliation, she had time for something. She was radiant and vital.

The laughter was a balm for her soul.

But as they exchanged stories, Viv knew that none of them really knew about fatigue the way she did. Or the dark question of whether being tired meant something worse, devastatingly worse.

But, for the most part, Viv kept those thoughts at bay for the afternoon. Good food, great company, and belly laughs were a good defense against her darkness.

And she had gotten the scoop on her own daughter.

Siena was moving forward in life, and this was important. But it was also a necessity. There it was: the dark thought. Siena needed to move forward without Viv.

Chapter Fifteen

Siena

Irish Hills and Siena were up early and ready. It was June 15th.

Libby had explained that hosting "events" almost every weekend was part of her grand plan. From Memorial Day to Labor Day, she'd planned special reasons to come to downtown Irish Hills. But the real beginning of summer was now. It was finally time.

"Kids are out of school, the water's warmed up, the families are here, the renters are rotating in and out, it really is prime time," Libby explained.

Libby had lured businesses. She'd convinced other business owners to stay when they would have shut down and moved out. She'd fended off a billionaire development.

But if no one came to shop, eat, drink, or get their hair done in Irish Hills, it would be hard to claim victory. Irish Hills needed people to thrive, not just promises.

As early as Siena got in, fueled by nervous energy for the shop's opening day, Libby was already downtown, hard at work. She had an office set up across the street.

She called it phase two, and Dean Tucker was about to start renovations. There would be six more spaces for shops or restaurants when Libby was done. Siena had seen renderings, but even if she hadn't, Libby painted a picture with her descriptions of what Irish Hills could be in another year.

Libby arrived to give Siena one more '*atta girl* before they opened.

"Everything looks wonderful," Libby said. She walked through Siena's carefully displayed showroom floor.

"The classics are all here. These are the perennial pieces that built her brand."

The clothes were beautiful. They made women look sophisticated and helped them feel confident at the head of the boardroom table or at a cocktail party. Siena was proud of her mother, and she could see Libby was proud of both of them.

The pieces her mom had contributed for exclusive debut at the store were in the same vein. But she'd allowed some new summer colors.

Libby stopped at a clothes rack that Siena had struggled to integrate into the rest of the pieces.

"Oh, she's added the kaftan to her line!"

"Ha, no, those aren't Vivian Blackwood Designs. They're, uh, just no label craft projects. She has hand sewn almost one a day since she's been here. She is supposed to be resting; instead, she's making muumuus."

"I love them—do me a favor, ring this one up for me. Or put it aside? If you sell out and have to sell it, cool. But otherwise, I need this one. She had a lavender one on the other day that had me hating my stupid khaki shorts."

Libby did not look like the kaftan type. But Siena did what her new aunt asked.

"Wow, and the botanicals on the walls. I love those too."

"Ha, the décor isn't for sale, Aunt Libby, but next time I head to Tecumseh, I'll grab you some."

"Great, it's going to be great. You have help?"

"Yes, Alison Barton, she's great. She was working at Target, so she had retail experience. She is coming in. She's all trained. Two of us should be good for today."

"My Aunt Emma wants to help if you need it too. She loved selling last summer; my rich old aunt loves working a cash register. Who knew?"

"Thank you, I just don't have a good sense of how busy we'll be."

"Busy. This is the first really warm weekend. Memorial Day is great, but we're in summer now, well, more or less."

"You're a dynamo. All the Sandbar Sisters are. I'm sort of amazed. The victory you pulled off here…"

"Thank you, honey. Well, Stone Stirling likes to say I won, but he's lurking around. He bought the old Hudson place, and he's turned Irish Hills into his summer headquarters. He's conceding, but maybe he's just waiting for me to fail."

Siena did not see Aunt Libby failing at anything.

Siena clicked on a little light in the window. It glowed "Open."

"Here goes nothing," Siena said.

"It's awesome. And thank you, I know it's been hard with Viv. She isn't sold on this store idea, and you went out on a limb. One I had to keep you out on."

"I'm glad you did. I've loved setting this place up and having help from the Sandbar Sisters to cheer Mom up."

"She seems better, happier, I think."

"I think so, too."

"I'm glad you're here, and so is Cole, from what I gather." Libby winked at Siena.

She blushed. "We're just hanging out. I like him. Let's not get crazy."

"Oh, I'm going to get crazy. I plan to use you as an example to convince my kids that Irish Hills is the place to be. Luring country music stars here is one thing, but twenty-somethings I gave birth to? That's the real trick!"

"I don't know about me as an example. But use me how you need. I love this place."

She hoped the feeling was mutual. It was about time to see if the town and the tourists loved her back. Libby said foot traffic would likely start late in the morning.

"Getting up early to shop isn't a vacation vibe, but they'll still be here before lunch. I'll pop in later if I get a minute."

"Thanks, Aunt Libby."

Libby left, and Alison, her one and only employee, arrived. Vivian Blackwood Boutique was open for business and officially a part of Irish Hills. Siena's play to save her mom's life's work was underway.

She took a breath and straightened the table of scarves for the four-thousandth time.

Alison was at the checkout. Siena had outfitted Alison in a Vivian Blackwood pair of trousers and a silk blouse. If the concept took off, she'd be sure that all the employees were dripping in Vivian Blackwood Designs. Alison was a little shorter than Siena but still tall, with long legs. She looked great in the chic ensemble, but something was out of place. Siena couldn't put her finger on what. She chalked it up to first-day jitters.

"Remember, we want to wrap the garment in the tissue and then add tissue on top of the gift bag."

"I gotcha. Make it a gift even if someone's buying for themselves."

"Exactly."

As Libby predicted, their first customer walked in at 10:30 am. Not quite morning and not quite lunch.

Three ladies, who looked to be her mom's age, maybe a little older, slowly wound their way through the boutique.

"Welcome to Vivian Blackwood Boutique. Our newest pieces are along this wall, and the classics are right here. I'm Siena."

They nodded, and Siena gave them space. She hated to be hovered over when she shopped. It was a delicate mix of helping a customer and suffocating their experience.

She pretended to busy herself as she watched the women circle.

They passed the rack of blouses, the new blazers, and even the scarves. Siena had the scarves out as a "just in case" kind of thing. Just in case they didn't need bigger pieces but wanted a little Vivian Blackwood cache.

Siena was a little crestfallen as the women sniffed by each rack. Nothing she had on the racks was soliciting body language that suggested they'd even like to try something on.

Finally, a question from the first woman through the door.

"This print of the lilacs on the wall, how much? It really would be just the thing for my front hall."

Siena walked over and looked at the botanical watercolor that she'd purchased to warm up the space.

She did not have it on display to buy, but then she started calculating. She had five more in the back. She'd planned to rotate them in and out to keep the space fresh. Heck with it. She'd sell it. She doubled the price she'd paid for it at the Tecumseh Trade Center.

"Oh, that's wonderful. I'll take it."

"Lovely, we can wrap it up, and Alison can help you take it out to your car."

"Thank you so much."

Siena stepped over to the cash register.

"Alison, can you go get the step stool and get the painting for me. I'll ring this up."

The painting had no bar code and wasn't in their new system. Siena rang it up under miscellaneous and pretended that she had meant to sell the art. The customer was always right, right?

They packed the art, loaded it, and Siena retrieved a replacement from the storeroom, so the wall wouldn't be bare.

All the while, several shoppers came in, floated in circles around the store, and exited without buying a thing.

Crud.

But then, finally, a woman walked up with an actual garment.

"I'll take this, and this one too." The woman placed two of the kaftans that her mother had given her as an afterthought on the counter. Siena watched as Alison rang them up.

After four hours opened, they'd sold a picture off the wall and two kaftans.

"The ladies really liked the kaftans. That's great," Alison said.

"Yes, for sure." Siena wanted to inspire confidence in the sole employee she had in the store. So she pretended she wasn't feeling a stark panic in her chest. They weren't really planning to sell the kaftans, but Alison had mistakenly put them out, and Siena hadn't had the heart to put them in the back. Not after Libby had admired them. Ugh. Her plans were not working as she'd envisioned.

She pretended she'd expected this outcome. But she hadn't. Her idea for the retail store was to revitalize her mom's design business, not run it into the ground.

As she disguised her panic, another little scrum of nice ladies walked in and said no to the blazers, no to the scarves, and no to the tailored pants.

But then, a question.

"How much are you selling these table coverings for? They're just what I need in my cottage kitchen."

Siena did the same mental math. She wasn't planning on selling the décor she'd curated to make the store look warm and inviting but modern at the same time, but dang it if that's what the customer wanted, she'd sell it.

"Those are forty-nine-ninety-nine." This was three times what she'd paid. But she had to pay Alison, for crying out loud.

The woman didn't blink. "Great, I'll take this one. I love it."

Siena removed the stock off the table, swiped the table covering, and folded it. As she did, the ladies found the kaftan rack, and Alison rang up the table covering and two more kaftans.

"Thanks for coming in!" Siena said as they left.

"Wow, those kaftans are hot. How many do we have?"

"Ten, I had ten, so now, six left."

As the day wore on, the scene replayed.

She tried to hide that she was deeply worried. One day wasn't enough to know for sure if this was a bust, was it?

Finally, Cole came in with a takeout order of food for Siena and Alison.

They took turns eating, and Cole listened as she freaked out quietly in the back room. She didn't want her sole employee to regret leaving her old job at Target.

"It's like my mom's gorgeous designs are nothing. I haven't sold a single one. They're gorgeous, chic, powerful, and just all the things that women want. I can't understand it."

"Well, I mean, maybe it's the audience. Around here, it's flip-flops and tennis shoes."

"You're a fashion marketer now?"

"Sorry, you're right. What do I know? Just give it some time."

She realized she'd snapped at Cole, and he was just trying to help.

"No, I'm sorry, it's worry and panic talking. Nothing. I've sold nothing, and this was my idea to save Mom's business."

As she paced, Alison popped her head into the back room.

"Two more kaftans, we're down to four of those, and the replacement art, same price? A lady wants it."

"Yes, same price."

"See," Cole said, "you are selling the art, the kaftans, and didn't you say a tablecloth?"

"Yes, that will be enough to pay Alison for the day, but not for lunch."

"Lunch is on me."

Siena looked at Cole. He was just a good person. He had walked in as a favor to Aunt Libby and had done whatever she asked.

As unlucky as the store was looking right now, Cole Brady was the jackpot.

That idea calmed her down. That was good.

She'd hang on to that as she watched customer after customer pass on Vivian Blackwood Designs.

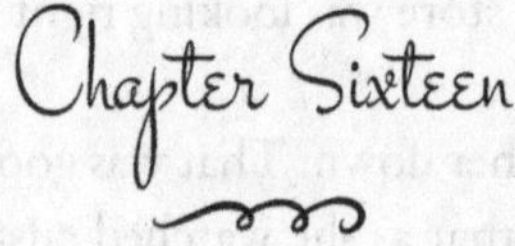

Chapter Sixteen

Viv

Viv had stayed away. She wanted Siena to fly on her own. She wanted her daughter to feel free to make decisions and to think about something other than taking care of her mother.

She had met Cole briefly when she'd swung by during all the prep work, but she wasn't going to get in their way. In the deepest part of her heart, she knew that Siena had to move forward in life.

Though Viv had resigned herself to the rest of her own life being filled with worry about the next call from the doctor, the trip to Irish Hills had been surprising.

She'd found relief from the constant oppressive thoughts. She'd even found a new creative energy. And truth be told, a new friend.

Larson Taggert was important to her. She didn't know how or what possible future they had, but for now, they enjoyed each other's company and seemed to understand each other.

Tag had asked her a favor for the day. He needed help, and she was the one to give it.

"I just need you to be a set of ears, you get it?"

"I get it."

The phrase had a double meaning. Yes, she could listen to the doctor and make sure he didn't miss something, but also, he was hard of hearing on one side. He said that was also the accident, an explosion right near his ear.

But today, it was about his leg. He was getting the boot off.

Viv knew what it was like to listen to a doctor, to hang on every word, and then miss half of them. The emotion, hope, and fear wrapped into every sentence made it hard to listen for understanding and to ask the questions to which you needed answers. Siena had done that for her, and she was going to do that for Tag.

They drove way too fast on the highway and sat in the offices of Dr. Marion Anderson on the campus of the University of Michigan. When it was Tag's turn, they were in her office, not the exam room.

"Doc, this is my friend Viv."

"*The* Vivian Blackwood! Wow, I'm honored."

"I didn't know you were famous," Tag said.

"I'm not, well, I am to women in impressive careers, like Dr. Anderson here." It was easy to see Dr. Anderson was an impressive professional.

"I wore your Power Suit when I interviewed for the department head job, and wow, the Means Business Blazer when I presented at a big conference a few years back."

"Well, it looks like it worked." The office walls had an impressive array of degrees. This was a woman on top of her game.

"I loved it. Okay, so Tag, there's good news and bad news." The doctor explained that Tag's surgery had gone well and that he'd be able to continue rehab and get to a point where he could walk without pain. It would take time, but she was confident his gait would be close to normal after PT.

"I'm headed for the bad news now, right?"

"Right, the crash, as you know, caused an explosion. That

explosion is why you're having hearing trouble in that left ear. I'm also concerned about it moving forward."

Tag swallowed. Viv could see his Adam's apple rise, his jaw clench.

Viv was here for a reason, so she reached out a hand to Tag, and he took it.

"What can you do for the hearing loss?"

"Not much. Honestly, nothing. And if you keep racing, it will get worse due to the nature of the sport."

Viv looked at Tag.

"The car is loud as heck, Viv, loud as heck."

"And you, my friend, didn't wear earplugs even before this."

"I know, I know."

"Could this impact his career?" Viv asked.

"Maybe. I'm sure you can drive with impaired hearing, but you're essentially deaf in that ear now, Tag. You keep driving, and you risk the hearing you have left in the other ear."

Viv squeezed Tag's hand. He squeezed back. She knew what he was going through, not the same thing, but close enough. He was getting life-altering news, and it was too much to process in one meeting.

The doctor outlined the rest of the results for Tag. He was in otherwise pretty great shape for a fifty-three-year-old man who'd been in several major wrecks during his career.

It was all good, except for the ear.

Dr. Anderson was reassuring and intelligent, and Viv thought if she lived here, she'd want her to be her physician. Tag was in good hands. The larger implications were something he'd need to think about.

But Viv was glad she was here to be his ears, for a bit anyway.

As they finished, Viv also noticed something else.

The doctor, impressive as she was, wasn't in a power suit or even in any formal wear. She wasn't in scrubs or anything; she was just casual. A pair of slacks and a cotton t-shirt under her white coat was it. She also had on cute tennis shoes. They were in an impressive office, but Dr. Marion Anderson wasn't dressed to the nines.

Viv decided to get more information, slyly, if she could.

"If you ever need to get a new Power Suit, it's on me," Viv offered the doctor.

"Oh, thank you, but you know, since I turned fifty these days it's all about comfort."

"I get it. You don't know how much." With comfort, maturity, and no longer needing to get the job, Dr. Anderson had the job. She didn't need to dress like other people. Viv mulled that over a little.

Tag drove them back. They were quiet for a time. He was processing the news that he was risking total deafness if he pursued the career he loved. It was a lot.

Finally, he looked over at her.

"You ready to let it rip?"

"What?"

"I'm going to blow through the speed limit on this last stretch of road. You ready?"

"I'm ready."

Music blaring, top down, Tag and Viv flew back to Irish Hills as if they didn't have a care in the world.

* * *

Tag headed back to his place, and Viv decided to spend some time at her sewing machine. She had no designs, no plans, just creative license to make her kaftans.

Tag's diagnosis had her thinking about the crossroads she was facing in her own career. Siena was doing all this work to fight for her company. She had pinned her hopes on a retail location and maybe even many retail locations, but Viv's lack of interest or will to get on board with the plan wasn't a defeat.

It was just time.

Viv picked a lovely little yellow piping from the supply she'd found at a secondhand store in Adrian. She pinned it along the collar. This one had a notched keyhole at the neck. All of her kaftans were different. They took shape organically. The colors and shapes and her mood dictated the final garment, not a pattern.

She looked at it. Assessed. Maybe it needed more room at the shoulders? She got lost in the design of this one item, this new art.

"Mom?"

Siena was at the door. She looked sad rather than keyed up like she'd been lately.

"Yes, love, come in."

Siena saw the current work in progress. "These are so pretty. This one is going to be yellow with a little red? My goodness, so far from Vivian Blackwood classics."

"These are just for fun."

"About that..."

"How did the big grand opening go?"

Siena came over and sat on the bed. In the last few months, she'd looked all grown up, ready to take on the world, and she'd offered her broad shoulders to her old mom.

But right now, Viv could see the sweet little girl. The furrow in her brow and the downturn of her lips made Viv think she was about to report that she was sad because someone was mean to her in her class.

That little girl was right there, just under the surface of the woman her daughter had become. Viv had been pushing hard to be sure Siena could stand on her own two feet, but suddenly she wanted to do the exact opposite. She wanted to take her hand and reassure her that she wasn't alone, that mom would take care of whatever was wrong.

"What is it?"

"It was a disaster."

Viv tilted her head. "I doubt it was that. The store was lovely. You made it so."

Siena was hesitating. Her daughter was holding back. And then it dawned on Viv why that might be.

"Are we saying there were no customers in the store disaster, or do you mean no one bought the designs disaster?"

Silence hung between them. That was the answer then. No one was buying Vivian Blackwood anymore.

Siena finally spoke. "There were customers. And they bought stuff, but not any of the career wear."

"What else could they have possibly bought then?"

"They bought six wall pieces I had hung to decorate the store. I was going to switch them out all season, so I had stock of them for us. As soon as I put one up, it would sell."

"Ooh, that artist is hot then," Viv said.

"That's the thing, there were a variety of artists."

"Hmm."

"And they bought these table coverings, tablecloths, that I had put on the display tables. I didn't even have prices on them, and they were grabbing them. I didn't want to sell them, but I figured at least I could pay Alison with the cash from that."

"It's a store. I'd say if they want to buy anything from soup to nuts, it's for sale." Viv tried to take a light tone. She didn't want Siena to be so serious, so forlorn over the first day of the store.

"But Mom, this was my best idea for saving the business. Not one suit jacket or scarf. I thought we had this new retail idea, and it would reinvigorate everything. It was my big idea."

Things that Viv had been noticing, in the background, on the periphery, came into sharp focus. The problem was easy to see now. It was obvious where they had been oblivious.

"Honey, the big idea was my clothing line. And that was decades ago. The time is up for it. It's not the big idea anymore."

"What? People love your clothes. You're a ground-breaking

designer. You made career wear for women what it is. I'm so tired of you just giving up on things. You're fine. The cancer is gone."

Siena had gone from down in the mouth to actually crying. This isn't what Viv had intended.

"Honey, this isn't me giving up. It's me seeing it, really seeing it. It's time for me, for us, to close Vivian Blackwood Designs." The isolated things she'd noticed added up in her mind. Viv tried to sort through them and explain to Siena what was clear. "Honey, listen, it's coming to me now, exactly the problem. Why I can't even design what I used to. The need just isn't there for my designs. Women my age have moved on, and younger women don't need the stuff."

"What are you saying younger women aren't career-minded? That's ridiculous!"

She tried to explain another way. "No. Okay, look. I took Tag to the doctor today. She was my age, and she loved my designs when she was coming up. When she was interviewing for her big jobs. But she was wearing a t-shirt and tennis shoes in her office today."

"That's one person. I don't get it."

"Okay, look at someone like Libby. She was, in my mind's eye, the model for my Power Suits and career separates. She told me she owns one, one complete outfit from me these days, and that's because she's sentimental about it. We've been here weeks and in business settings, right? Think about it, she's powerful and in the prime of her career, but she walks around in blouses, sweatshirt material skirts, and even jeans. She's wearing a lot more casual than I ever would have imagined for my avatar career woman. She's in charge, and she's wearing what she wants."

"I think I sort of see what you're saying..."

"I'm saying the career women who made my brand are my age. They're in their fifties. They want something new. They've got what they need from me, or they're starting to work from home or change careers or become grandmas. They do not want baby spit on their Vivian Blackwood sheath dress."

"Mom, what are we going to do? How can we save all you've worked for?"

"Honey, I love you for all you've done to keep it going in the last year. But it's time to stop. It's run its course. It's time to close up Vivian Blackwood Designs. Financially, we're just fine. Thanks to Daddy's smart decisions with the investments, we are set. I don't need much to live on, and your college is paid for. It's okay."

Siena's shoulders slumped, but she seemed calmer, like she was accepting the reality, and it wasn't terrifying. It was just a change.

"Mom, we're committed to that retail space. I promised Aunt Libby. I want something to work there. I just, ugh. What a mess."

"Well, you did make sales. The décor and the painting. What if—"

Before she could finish her question, Siena cut her off. "— What if we pivot. What if I stock it with home décor?"

"Right, and this is a resort town. They don't want business casual; they want casual casual. You get it?"

"I see that. I'm also thinking how dumb I was not to see it right away."

"You have an eye for merchandising and a degree for it. Use it to break away from my stuff."

"I love your stuff."

"Honey, it's time for *your* dream. Don't worry about my dreams. Okay?"

"Okay."

Viv hugged her daughter. She looked at Siena's pretty face, so much like Goldie's. Viv noticed that the frown line on Siena's forehead smoothed out as the new idea blossomed.

"There, okay, I'll call your dad, and we'll see what needs to be done to close up, liquidate, whatever we need to do."

"Oh, you know what did sell out of yours?"

"I thought you said nothing?"

"I forgot. The kaftans, we sold every single one, and I have a list of a dozen women who wonder if you'll be making more."

"You're joking!"

"Nope, so get sewing. I've got to go find cool stuff for the store. I need to head to that flea market again, and I heard there's one in Detroit, too, that I need to check out, the Eastern Market, and then I need to see if Cole can drive me to another place in Toledo that's not too far."

Siena was going a mile a minute again.

She was making plans.

Siena had hope. She had excitement. She'd bounced back from a bad day.

Ah, to be so young.

Siena was off to make calls. Viv sat back at her sewing machine. She touched the fabric of the current creation.

Kaftans? Who knew?

Chapter Seventeen

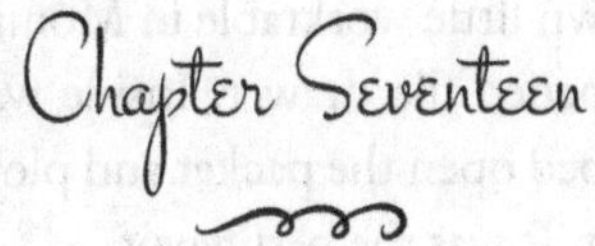

Siena 2006

The model stood still, like a statue. Siena looked up at her in awe. She was like a princess. She was Belle or Ariel!

Her mother swirled pretty fabric around. Momma's two assistants pinned things together. The two took her mother's directions.

"Shorter here, no, a little looser at the shoulder, like this." Momma leaned in and adjusted the fabric.

"Momma, can I get a snack?"

Momma never ignored her or scolded her when she asked questions. She learned about colors and bias cuts and darts and just all sorts of things. All she ever had to do was ask.

Momma turned to look at her and then came over and kneeled down.

"I know this has lasted longer than I thought it would. Daddy's still at the office and said he'll bring home some pizza. Does that sound good?"

"Yes, but I am still hungry now."

"Why don't you go over to your drawing table. I have a little treat for you in the drawer. If you draw a little, I promise I'll be done, and it will be pizza in no time!"

"Okay."

Siena had her own little worktable in Momma's studio. She sat on the stool and opened the drawer. Inside was a packet of fruit snacks. Yay! She ripped open the packet and plopped the red one in her mouth. Red first. It was the best flavor.

There were also new pencils.

Siena took the colored pencils and began to do her own sketching. Sort of like Momma, but not of dresses or models. Siena liked to draw pictures of the rooms she was in.

Siena did her best to draw what she saw in the office.

But she decided the walls were too boring, so she drew a picture on the wall. A picture on the picture! This idea made her laugh. She drew some flowers into the empty corner. And before she knew it, her paper was filled with color.

She didn't know how much time had passed, but Momma came over.

"All done with work. Daddy called, pizza on the way!"

"Good, I'm still hungry," Siena said.

Her mother paused and looked at the drawing.

"Siena, this is the studio?"

"Yes, well, it started as that. I don't know what it is now."

"A flowerpot there, a picture there, and what's that?"

"That's a poof chair, like my room. I think there should be more poof in here, less sharp."

"I think so too. That would be just the thing! Let's take your drawing from today and show Daddy at dinner, sound good?"

"Yep.'"

Momma carefully tore the drawing off the pad.

"Put your pencils back so you have them the next time."

Siena did as her mother asked.

The drawing made its way to the dining room with them. Daddy also thought it was a good job.

It earned a place on the refrigerator, and then, the next day, Momma took her to an outdoor market. It wasn't like the department stores; it was more like a fair or a carnival.

They bought whatever Siena liked. They walked and walked.

Everything they bought wound up in Momma's studio. Her picture came to life!

Siena Present

Cole was behind the wheel again, and Siena was thinking about her mom's studio.

The studio had morphed over time into the picture Siena had drawn, and her mom had hung on the fridge. A lot of the rooms did, Siena would imagine it and her parents made it real. She knew that was unique, she knew that her parents encouraging her creatively was a gift. But somehow, she always thought her creativity had to fold into her mother's.

Why start again? Why not bolster the family business? It just made sense. It was logical in Siena's mind. And while both her parents encouraged her, they were happy, thrilled even, when she wanted to work for the Vivian Blackwood business.

She loved design, but not clothing design. Her childhood drawings, the new direction of the store, was this her calling? She loved making the space look a certain way, not making a person look a certain way.

Siena was invigorated with the idea that instead of just background objects, she was going to find things that she loved to decorate with, and that, maybe, would be the way to turn the store into a success.

"You're a million miles away," Cole pointed out.

"A million years, more like."

"What are you thinking?"

"My mom's old studio, how she decorated it based on my childhood scribbles."

"See, you had a good eye even then. Is that what they say, 'good eye'?"

"Yeah, I guess so. It's just I've been so focused on my mom's fashions, the idea that I'd have a totally different concept for the store, well, it's a lot to think about."

"Seems to me you're already good at it."

"Thanks, but what the heck? I even need a new name."

"I suppose so."

"Maybe Vivian Blackwood Home or Vivian Blackwood Accents?"

"I'm sure you'll think of the right thing. Ooh, there's a spot."

Cole parked the truck. It was time to see if her good eye could turn the store from a miss to a hit.

Viv

For all the business decisions she'd ever made, Bret had been there. He was there when she had nothing but a sketchbook and an attitude. He was there when she sent her first collection down the runway. He was there when her designs were featured in Goldie's movie. And there when the First Lady wore Vivian Blackwood Designs to the State of the Union.

So, it was natural, after the decision she'd made to end Vivian Blackwood Designs, to call Bret. As was her habit, she got right to her point with no chit-chat.

"What do we need to do to close up?" That was her question.

"No, hi Bret, how are you? What's it like in New York State without my beautiful daughter and morose ex-wife? Oh, fine, thank you, but less fun? And you?"

"I'm morose?"

"Kind of, yes. I was hoping Siena's little plan would change that. How's it going?"

"Different than I thought, but I think I've convinced our daughter that the end is here for my career wear."

"Hmm, the end, you say?"

"I wasn't paying attention, and things moved on."

"You were otherwise occupied. Are you sure? We did a lot of cost-cutting. We did things to keep it afloat. You sold your house. There's liquidity there if you need more time. And, of course, you have plenty of personal money."

Viv knew she had money to live comfortable for the rest of her life. More than enough since the plan was for her to live to her seventies or eighties. She decided against pointing out he'd overshot the estimate on the rest of her life. Bret had already called her out on being morose.

"I'm glad I had good business advice."

"I'm good like that," Bret said.

She thought about his word, time, more time. She did need more time, but not for this part of her life. "I think time is actually the point. The time is over for the kind of stuff I've been designing."

"Honey, the stuff you created is classic, and let's just be clear on that."

"You don't have to assuage my ego. I am okay with being out of fashion or out of touch with the new generation of, what do they call them, girl bosses?"

"That's out too."

"Man, I do have one foot in the grave."

"See? Morose, knock it off."

"Okay, yeah, that sounded bad."

Bret and Viv didn't have an explosive breakup. But their romance shifted into friendship after the initial realization that Bret loved her, but he was in love with Trevor. As their love life evaporated, their business took root.

And they'd always been on the same parenting page with Siena. They were tied together, forever, with Siena. And they because they'd built Vivian Blackwood Designs together. The marriage ended, the bond didn't. The best parts about them as a couple remained, even if the couplehood didn't. She'd been sad when their marriage ended, but never bitter. Bret would always be a blessing in her life. Who said the love of your life couldn't be your best friend?

Viv was finding that to be true for her, and she was grateful.

"I can't begin to know how this all feels, but are you sure? We could probably keep it going."

"The thing is. I don't want to. You know? I think my life, even my creative self, is going somewhere else."

"Where's that?"

"You're going to laugh."

"I'll try not to," Bret said.

"Siena is going to pivot the store from my career designs and do home décor."

"You know I LOVE THAT! I mean, how many times did we have to reimagine her bedroom décor based on her new ideas?"

"Right?" Viv recalled moving beds and dressers and buying new paint a couple times a year.

"And with that merchandising degree, this makes so much sense."

"Right and untethering her from my business is the way to go. She needs to fly."

"Agree, but fly with you in town, right? You're going to be there, right?"

"Yeah, seeing as I don't have a house anymore. I may buy something here just to be around for Siena as long as I can. She can have it after."

"Ugh, after a good long time. But good. Okay, none of this makes me laugh at you. You said I would laugh. What's that about?"

"I'm designing kaftans, that's it."

"What? Like muumuus?"

"Yes, flowy, colorful, flattering, diva-esque, no-shapewear-required kaftans."

"Did you do market research? Is there a need or a gap in the retail space for tent dresses?"

"Stop it. No. No research. I just discovered a vintage one, and that was it. I got focused."

"Oh, like before?"

Bret had seen Viv when she would forget to eat, shower, and take bathroom breaks because she was so intensely focused. He'd been there when she'd forgotten to pay the electric bill in her tiny apartment because who had time for anything but design. He'd been there to help her do what she loved. It was another reason she loved him. He was a giving person, and he'd given so much to her. She wished she could give him more, but he always said she was his family. She gave him family.

Viv felt tears well in her eyes, thinking of the family, the life they'd built.

"Yes, like before." She answered his shorthand language question. Like before, is the answer only two people with history understand.

"I'm not laughing then. You do this. I'll get the business shuttered. There's a matter of inventory to deal with. None of the top-line stores will want close out. But there are other outlets."

"No."

"What?"

"I want to give them away. All of it."

"What, to like Goodwill?"

"Yes, you said we don't need the revenue, right?"

"True. It's better for our tax obligation to donate, not profit."

"Well, my motivation is women not taxes. I want women to be able to order an interview suit from us. We'll ship it to her for free."

"You're going to have people buying a ton and then reselling, making money off your good intentions."

"I know we'll have to figure out a way around that, but that's what I want to do. If you need a suit, you come to Vivian Blackwood Designs online, and we'll send it to you. If you need to nail that job interview or promotion or look good when you have to go to court to testify against your ex. Whatever it is. Maybe it is one per address unless the address is a women's shelter."

"You're something else, Ms. Blackwood."

"Thanks, you too, Mr. Blackwood. So, you can handle that end? Figure out how to set it up?"

"I can, but what about these kaftans? Do you want me to grab a few of the buyers and run that up the flagpole? I'd need a few pictures and sketches; you know the drill. I can see if there's interest. They might find some space for your new direction on the racks for spring."

"No. Vivian Blackwood is no more. The designs I'm doing are just for me. For my own outlet. Do you get it?"

"Okay, okay, but your daughter and I love a good merchandise idea."

"Shh, just roll up the sidewalk, okay?"

"Okay, I'll call you back once I do some research on the give-away idea."

"Okay, and Bret?"

"Yeah, love?"

"Thank you, thank you for all of it. I know darn well I'd be in that dark apartment with my sketchbook and a box of macaroni and cheese if it wasn't for you. You made this dream come true."

"We're a team and thank you. And stop being so maudlin. I can't take it."

"Okay, got it."

They ended the call. With Bret handling the shutdown, Viv had that off her mind.

Viv called Tag. "How about you give me a ride downtown? If you're not doing anything."

"Just arguing with my insurance company. I can do that later. I'll be over in a few minutes."

"Thanks."

Viv and Tag were in a similar spot in life, caught between the end of one career and the future. Neither of them was sure what the next stretch of life was going to be like. If someone told her a year ago that she'd be back in Irish Hills, hanging out with the Sandbar Sisters and quasi-dating a race car driver, she would not have believed it.

But she'd been able to be more herself here than she'd been in the last year, especially with Tag. Maybe that's what she liked about him. He accepted her sometimes less-than-sunny disposition and didn't ask that she fake it. She didn't need to be brave with him, just herself.

He could laugh when she made a dark joke. He'd been to some dark places of his own after his accident.

She heard his arrival before she saw it. The convertible roared into the front of the hotel.

Viv loved the gaudy thing. The air, the noise, the half-crazy way Tag drove, all of it woke her up from the haze of being seen as a patient, not a person.

He hadn't talked about his visit to the doctor. Or too much about his diagnosis, and that was okay. She knew what it was like to make health the center of every conversation. Some days it felt like her cancer had become the most important thing. What did she think about if not that?

She walked out of the car and got in. It was a familiar spot for her now.

"So, you'd kept your hands off of the store, but here we are going downtown. What's changed?"

"I can be supportive and not the boss, and it's hers now, really hers. This isn't a boutique of my designs. It's her vision."

"Makes sense."

Viv leaned back in her seat. Summer was here. It was the part of summer she loved, June. The entire season was ahead. They had the fun and celebration of July to look forward to and the heat of August to revel in, but right now, it was the beginning. She liked this, being at the beginning. Viv had been thinking and talking about endings so much lately.

The end of her treatment, the end of her business, and maybe the end of—no, not going there. She was going to work hard to be in the moment. And this moment was about beginnings.

"Wow, this town has never looked this good!"

They pulled into Irish Hills, and though it was a weekday, the busy weekend still to come, there were flowers blooming in vases, people strolling in and out of the few businesses, and Dean Tucker was across the street, supervising the next phase of Libby's grand plans. This was a symphony of beginnings. No wonder Siena had been convinced to be a part of Irish Hills. Viv felt the energy and wanted to be a part of it too.

"Looks like the sign is being repainted."

Tag parked a few spaces away from the store. A crew was covering her name with paint.

"Is that a bad omen?" she asked as Vivian was obscured and they worked on Blackwood.

"Ackwood, I could just call you that from now on. Let's check out the inside of the store, Ackwood."

"No, that's not my nickname. I forbid it."

"No one can pick their nickname. That's a law."

"Oh, really?"

Tag reached out and took her hand. Hand-holding was about all she could deal with. It was the right speed for her. The race car driver let her set that pace.

They walked into the space and found Siena. She was on a ladder placing several items on a high shelf.

"Ugh, see, kids today do not understand they need someone to hold the ladder." Tag went over and did the honors. He was moving pretty well, with no boot or crutch.

"Thanks, Mom. So glad you're here! I've got so much to do."

"I think it looks like you've got too much to do."

Boxes were half unpacked and all over the store.

"I've gotten most of the old stock removed...ugh, well, not old, but you get it."

"I do."

"Most of the new stuff is in the back, here. Let me show you."

As chaotic as the front of the store appeared, the back was twice that.

"Okay, there's a method, I swear."

Siena showed them vases, wall hangings, faux greenery, plates, throw blankets, and on and on.

"I've got to get the old boxes out before I can get the new stuff in. Your kaftans are going to move up front, and I've got a table of accessories to pair with them. But that's pretty much the only clothing section."

"My kaftans?"

"Yep, if you don't want them to be labeled Vivian Blackwood, come up with another name because I am selling them as fast as you can sew 'em."

Viv hadn't thought about it as a business. She'd been doing it for fun, for a creative outlet. That a few people bought her new creations was nice, but a business? A new name?

"Honey, I'm sure that we've probably exhausted the people's interest in my kaftans at this point."

"Nope, every day, someone comes in here and wants to know when I'm getting more. Along with the question, what is this place? I really bungled the launch. But we're on track now. It will be clear; we have a focus."

"Okay, so what's the name you've decided on?"

"Just The Thing Shop." Siena cocked her head to the side as though she was still not sure of the name.

"I love it!"

"You used to say it to me when you let me accessorize your office or the sitting room."

"I did, that's right."

"I heard a few customers say that, too, about some of the things here."

"Honey, it's perfect! So cute!"

Her daughter's instincts were rock solid. Viv knew she wanted her approval, but honestly, she didn't need it. What she did need was help to get the store transitioned. Not help in what to buy or what to feature, but literal help packing and unpacking boxes.

"Good thing she likes it," Tag said. "Looks like the painter is half done out there outlining it on the sign."

Viv turned to Tag.

"How about you come to get me in a few hours?"

"What?" Tag turned his good ear to her, and she explained.

"I'm staying with her and helping her get this done."

"Hmm, you are weak as a kitten. What if I help too?"

"How could she say no? We're offering two middle-aged assistants with three ears, three legs, and no boobs between them."

"We're cheap. That's got to count for something," Tag quipped.

"We're a bargain at any price," Viv said. And she kissed Tag on the cheek. He pretended to fan himself. Viv laughed. He made her laugh.

Siena, who had whirled in and out of the space half a dozen times in as many seconds, whirled back in.

"Okay," Viv told her, "You've got Hopalong Taggert and the Cancer Queen ready to help."

"Mother." Siena didn't like her joke. Tag chuckled though.

"Oh, it's fine, we're here for a few hours, boss us."

"Are you sure?"

"Yes. How about we box up the rest of the career wear? We can put it in the back. And then I've got plans for it, actually. I'll have it picked up."

"What?" Siena asked the question, but she also seemed ready to move on to the next project of the million she was engaged in at the moment.

"Don't worry."

"Okay, yeah, get the stuff boxed up. That would help."

Viv folded clothes and Tag taped boxes shut. It took about an hour, but by the end, Siena had a blank slate for the main showroom to repurpose the space.

As the day wore on, Libby popped in, and so did J.J. They marveled at Siena's concept.

"This is it, really it is. I mean, the mercantile is all well and good for the necessities, cook wear, and such, but this place is class, all style!" J.J. said as she, too, pitched in to help hang three prints on the wall where blouses used to be.

As the day turned to evening, a call from Hope alerted them that she'd saved them a space at the counter for dinner.

"Sweet relief, I'm starving," said Tag. It was the first complaint he'd issued in a day of doing a million little things for Viv and her daughter.

Viv was struck again. She'd lucked into finding a wonderful person to add to her circle. She may not be headed for marriage with Larson Taggert but he, as they say, was good people. What luck?

Siena locked up the store, and the four of them walked over to Hope's.

They'd earned their appetites. And Viv sunk into the plate Lila put in front of her.

Her body was good tired for the first time in a long time. She'd moved it a lot today, and she'd helped her daughter instead of the other way around.

Not one dark thought slipped into her mind as she thought of what tomorrow might bring. Helping Siena launch Just The Thing was...just the thing.

Chapter Nineteen

Siena

She was just about ready. Siena was set to flip the store sign to open. For the first time it would be Just The Thing, not Vivian Blackwood Boutique.

The window display had a few of her mom's kaftan creations. The garments were a hot commodity. Her mother was so talented. It was good not to be in that shadow but try something different.

Siena smiled when she saw the tag her mother had sewn into each of the garments she'd made for the re-opening.

Viv and Breathe.

Siena felt like that was as good a sign as any that her mother was moving forward. The vitality that had been missing had started to reappear for longer and longer periods.

It made Siena feel lighter too, and as she arranged the last kaftan before she moved to the next task, she almost started to cry. It was not the plan she'd made when they'd set out for Irish Hills, but it was working!

Siena would sell the kaftans, maybe a shawl or two, and

perhaps even things to wear on the deck or boat. But she would focus on the home more than the clothes. That was what the customers had shown that they wanted from this store. But it was an experience more than just a store. After the redesign, she'd transformed her store from four walls and a cash register into a magical place. She felt it. She wanted her customers to feel it too.

Her store. She was amazed to hear herself call it that. The grand reopening wasn't grand in terms of fanfare. There were fliers up at the mercantile, and every diner at Hope's got a little coupon for a free bud vase if they visited Just The Thing.

But Siena wanted it to be a soft launch. She wanted to have time to see if people responded well and to fix what didn't work.

She did move the open time to nine am. People wanted to shop in the morning and get out on the water early. Ten, her original opening time, was too late—on a sunny day, at least.

She made coffee and had pastries for sale. If Libby could get a bakery in the downtown area, she'd do a deal with them, but for now, a nice cup of coffee and scone were there for people as they browsed.

She'd toyed with the idea of rainy-day hours and sunny-day hours, but that was one of many ideas she'd yet to implement.

For now, it was the traffic flow that interested her. She watched the customers filter in and paid close attention to how they inter-acted in her space. Alison was at the register, and today at least, her mom was there, gently welcoming visitors.

"No hard sell. Just let them browse." She'd told her mom the same thing she'd told Alison.

If the store was set up right, they'd be in the palm of her hand without realizing it.

Now, there were pockets of people slowly moving through the store. Siena had crafted a journey.

It was a good-sized space, and she wanted customers to travel through it in a specific way. They would see visions for the entryway of the home: a bench and the trays she'd found for muddy boots were on display. Each item she loved was staged in a way for customers to see how they could do the same in their homes.

She had a large section for kitchen and dining décor. There were no cooking supplies. They could find that at the mercantile. But linens, vases, and small prints in gold frames showed how a kitchen space could be personalized, warm, and inviting.

The customers then migrated to cozy spaces for reading or watching TV, or just sitting. Siena displayed pillows, more of the lap blankets that had sold on the first day, and a lovely lamp she'd thrifted and repurposed.

There was a small section of powder room accessories, and the handmade cachets she'd found were responsible for filling the store with a slight scent of lilac.

Finally, the bedroom items she'd curated had everything from duvet covers to adorable dishes for jewelry or your reading glasses. She imagined the dream lake cottages of her customers. It was at the front of her mind as she selected inventory.

It wasn't done, this store, and maybe it never would be. It was supposed to move and change with the way people lived here in Irish Hills. That was her dream, at least.

Her dream.

She'd never really pursued her dream. She'd always seen her dreams as a side note. She'd watched her big career woman mom and was happy that her life could fold into that. It was a family business, after all. And she had enjoyed it. She'd learned how her dad managed the business side at the same time as watching her mother's creative ideas turn into products.

They were both important and had come in handy when she'd decided to pivot. Siena had a sure hand and didn't vacillate. She knew what items would be perfect for the shelves of Just The Thing.

Cole had said he appreciated shopping with her because when she saw what she liked, she acted.

He'd told her so last night as she checked things one last time before the opening.

"My last girlfriend couldn't take a single step without texting her friends a picture. And she needed constant reassurance. I haven't once seen you take a selfie. That's all she seemed to do when we went anywhere."

Siena had still been at the beginning of what Cole had just said.

"Last girlfriend? I'm your current girlfriend?" She'd caught Cole. They were spending a lot of time together, but he'd said girlfriend. Were they official?

She was teasing him, but he was serious.

"Yes. That's how it is." Cole had looked into her eyes. They hadn't so much as held hands in the times they'd spent together. But he'd reached out, pulled her in at the waist, and kissed her softly, but with no doubt that yes, he considered her his girlfriend.

She'd leaned back and looked at his handsome face and the twinkle in his eye. "Yes, that is how it is. But you're my boyfriend." She'd put her arms up around his neck and kissed him right back.

It was a dreamy moment on top of her new dream store. She blushed a little now as she remembered it.

Then Alison's voice with an urgent question brought her back to the present.

"A lady on the phone wants to know if we are the store that carries the linen tablecloths she saw at her friend's house. We have three, she wants me to reserve one."

"Get her name and I'll set one aside." Siena loved going the extra mile to make customers happy. Hopefully that made the woman on the phone a customer for life.

As the door opened on Just The Thing, Siena's eyes were wide.

She realized she didn't just have a customer. She had a ton of them! And they were lined up to get in.

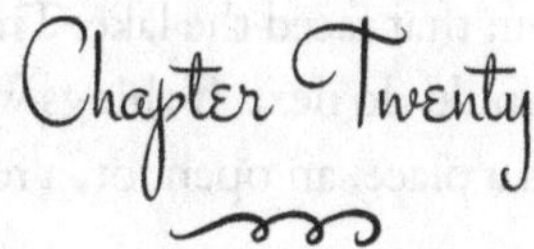

Chapter Twenty

Viv

The feeling started right before the re-opening. It was dull and distant.

Viv ignored it.

It was a low moan then. As if there was something howling in the night, far away, but stalking her. It was getting closer.

She ignored it. No reason to do anything but enjoy Siena's big day.

And it was a big day. Her daughter sold so much on day one—the kaftans were gone along with the art she'd procured and just about every bit of linen she had stocked.

They had a wonderful celebratory dinner by the water. This time it was at Hope's cottage after closing. They had leftovers and cold drinks.

Viv met Greg Macqueen; he already knew Tag. This was a small town, and that fact was charming, but Viv sometimes forgot how connected people were here.

Viv imagined this was the kind of cottage she could live in if things were different. She didn't need Nora House or Two Lakes Grove Hotel. Those places were grand. She had grand back in New York.

But a little cottage by the water. Something simple, with a light-filled sewing room that faced the lake. That would be lovely.

That's what she would do next. If things were different.

Tag said there was a place, an open lot, a few doors down from his fixer upper.

She promised to look at it, but the idea of buying or building was hopeful. It seemed like denial, planning that far ahead, when her future was uncertain at best, short at worst.

Because things weren't different. They were the same. The exact same as when they'd left New York and come here.

When the excitement of the relaunched store was over, she got on the phone with Marion Anderson. It was better to know for sure than to walk around in doubt. She did have plans to make. And she would make them herself. Not Siena. Not her doctors. Not Bret.

Viv was deciding her next steps on her own. And she'd do it armed with the truth. Positive thinking wouldn't change the science. She wanted the science. Then she'd figure out the rest.

The doctor was so nice and happy to help her. She ordered new tests.

"And I'll have your charts sent over from New York, yes, of course. It will give me the complete picture."

"How fast should I get the tests you're ordering?"

"Sooner is always better. I'll be here tomorrow. You get in at noon, and I'll see you in the afternoon. I'll pull some strings."

"That's, that's very sweet."

"Are you kidding? You're a legend. We're going to get you in here, and we'll get this handled."

"I, uh, I don't know what to say."

"Try not to worry. It's going to be fine."

She was oddly not worried. She was resigned. Viv had believed this would happen, and it was happening. She had an ache in the back of her ribcage.

She knew what it was. She *knew*.

But before she had it in black in white, she was going to take the day off.

Siena was out with Cole. Tag was in Detroit, meeting with his racing team, and Viv was free to do what she had done back in her youth.

The Sandbar Sisters were going to float all day. Goldie, J.J., and Viv had a date on the raft at Nora House.

Viv wore her newest kaftan, a flowy chiffon that happened to be the same color as her stylish mango sandals. She packed a change of clothes, a sweatshirt and shorts for if she got cold, and four more kaftans crafted especially for her friends.

She had a sensible Lands End one-piece bathing suit on under the kaftan. It covered everything, didn't ride up, and looked more athletic than matronly, she hoped. But in the end, she didn't really care. So much of her life had been designing and selecting the right clothes to impress or intimidate. Today, and since she'd been in Irish Hills, she wanted ease. She wanted flow. Her current ensemble did the trick.

Viv also arranged to have her own car. She'd called the local rental place, told them what she wanted, and it was here. She would drive herself to Libby's, and tomorrow she'd drive to the University of Michigan.

Siena didn't have to be her mother's hearse driver anymore.

Viv was the last to arrive at Nora House. Viv wanted to joke that she was the late Vivian Blackwood but decided Tag would think it was funny, but her girlfriends might scold her for being dark. She amused herself with the line but didn't speak it.

Viv let herself in through the kitchen.

The Sandbar Sisters were all on the back porch. The day was going to be warm and sunny, the perfect day to catch rays on the raft.

Before she walked out to them, she paused to remember another moment, back in 1989. Memories flooded back to her more and more each day. She let them come.

They were easier than what was next.

Viv 1989

Viv was decked out in her own creation.

Brock Lancaster had asked her to the fireworks at the club, and she wanted to make a splash. He was the coolest thing going this summer on Lake Manitou.

He belonged to the Irish Hills Country Club. Libby was the only one Viv knew who actually belonged to the club. Goldie said it was for old money gentile types. Viv had no idea what that meant. Goldie had lived here forever too, so she should know. J.J. said her mom could barely afford the "claptrap" they called home, no way could they afford Irish Hills Country Club. Hope's family were farmers. They, too, had no interest in the fancy club.

But Viv did have an interest. Her dad deposited them here in the summer and left. He wasn't into golf or even summer. And her mother spent the summer sunning with her friends. Her mom said, "go outside and play," but what she really meant was, "leave me alone."

That was fine by Viv.

Viv wanted to go to one of the fancy socials. She had an idea of what was in style and what looked cool, but she didn't have the actual experience of having a reason to dress up. This was an actual date, and she was going to go to the club with Brock Lancaster.

She had to pinch herself. Brock had shown up to Irish Hills this summer, and they all had a crush on him. Goldie liked to say he looked like John Taylor from Duran Duran. She was right. He had that kind of smile. Viv's knees felt like Jell-O anytime she saw him.

Somehow, he'd noticed her and asked her to this dance.

Hanging out with Libby, who looked like a model, and Goldie, who looked like a toothpaste commercial, Viv was not the first one a boy would notice. Which, up until last summer, she could not care less about. But then she got a crush on Todd Stromway, and he totally didn't know she was alive. She liked Randy Barton, but he used her to meet Goldie. Total loser.

Finally, this summer, Brock Lancaster paid attention. Viv knew she looked cute in her new bathing suit when they first met Brock out on the lake. And she also knew that Libby had a boyfriend, Hope was not interested in "lake guys," and J.J. was just too much of a cut-up to take any dating idea seriously. Luckily, Goldie was home sick the day they crossed paths with Brock. All the stars had aligned, and Brock Lancaster asked her if she wanted to go to the club dance and then watch the fireworks.

Yes. Yes, she did. And she knew just what she was going to wear.

Viv had always loved to sew. At first, it was adding bows to things or learning how to turn something baggy into something that fit her exactly. She added drawstrings and pleats. She used her mom's castoffs to create something new. By the time she was ten, she had her own sewing machine. By twelve, she learned how to sketch an idea and create a pattern.

She'd made all her friends terrycloth swim cover-ups. She'd taken every sewing class that they offered at Joann Fabrics. By fifteen, she could teach just about any sewing class at Joann Fabrics.

For a real date at the country club, she had more ideas than she ought to about what to wear. She was keen to show Brock Lancaster that she was worldly, stylish, and not a teenager who'd actually not been anywhere or done anything.

Her outfit was fashion-forward. While everyone would likely

be wearing puffy sleeves and dropped, waste dresses, Viv would not. She had a satin sheath; she'd created the sleeves and shoulders with sheer netting that matched the sheath. She'd tailored it to her small frame. Puffy overwhelmed her, and she knew it. She chose navy blue as the color. She had a black choker that her mom used to wear in the 1970s and attached the sheer netting to it to make it part of the dress. There wasn't a poof or a sequin to be found. It skimmed her body and fell at the perfect spot between her knees and ankles. She was so proud of her work!

She loved the look and knew it was her own style. No one would be in this dress because she hadn't gone to Jacobson's or the mall to get it. It was her creation.

Brock picked her up in his Fiero, which was the fanciest car in Lenawee County. He was in a sport coat, so that's how you knew this was a big deal! Normally, he was shorts and polo shirts.

He told her she looked pretty.

They joked about how they both thought the *Karate Kid III* was the dumbest movie ever, and when they got to Irish Hills Country Club, Brock politely offered to get her a glass of punch. She accepted, and he went off.

That's when it all went wrong.

She heard laughing behind her. It was a party, of course, and people were laughing. She ignored it, but when people are directing meanness toward you, you can feel it. It creeps across your skin, no matter how much you tried to pretend it wasn't directed at you.

Viv could feel it. Her neck was hot. She knew the laughter of the girls behind her was for her. Just in case she didn't, they got louder and aimed some remarks directly at her.

"Probably a Girl Scout sewing merit badge project."

They made comments that they could see her panty lines, her shoes were too cheap, and they hated her hair. She had it parted in the center and smoothed back. The girls at the club were still sporting Statue of Liberty bangs. Viv knew that wasn't "in" anymore in New York, but the club girls did not.

Viv didn't turn around. That probably infuriated them. She'd ignore it. That was all she could do unless she wanted to get into a fight at this fancy place. They started in on how flat her hair was. She knew it was petty and that they were just dumb.

She stayed quiet but felt her knees shaking. Her stomach was sick. Where was Brock? She was weak, and they could sense it.

She did want to have their approval. That was what all this was about, looking cool at the stupid Country Club.

"People make their own homemade dresses because they can't afford anything else."

That was not why she did it. She loved designing clothes. If she said that, it would be stupid. What should she say? Should she run?

"Shut up, Kelly, you look like you just got kicked out of a dive bar in *Star Wars* in that thing. You should talk."

It was a familiar voice.

"Ugh, and that dress, Kerry, is that your mom's? Wow."

It was Libby Quinn, one of her best friends and a regular here, much to her own annoyance.

The girls giggling stopped. Libby Quinn was smarter, more stylish, more beautiful, and had more guts than anyone else in this town, much less anyone at this country club.

"Hey, Viv!" Libby brushed passed the gaggle of girls and put an arm around Viv.

"Hi, Libby."

The girls now stared daggers at both of them.

Brock returned with the punch in hand.

"Are you kidding? Is this your date?" one of the club girls asked Brock, paying no attention to Viv and Libby anymore. Brock looked like she'd asked him for the equation to solving a Rubik's Cube.

"You brought *her* here?" another girl added.

"Uh, she needed a ride."

What? Viv needed a ride. What? Was that all this was?

Libby shifted her gaze from the mean girls to Brock. "A ride?"

"Yeah, we live down the street."

Viv saw Brock get smaller, physically and in all other ways. She was an outsider in his little clique, and the minute it was pointed out to him, he'd buckled.

Viv took Libby's lead. She stood up straighter, and she pretended she was too cool for all of this. Libby had given her the roadmap to be gutsy too. "Libby, did you drive?"

"I did come myself, actually."

"This country club thing is lame. Let's bounce."

"Agree."

Viv turned on her heel, and Libby followed her lead. Libby was naturally tall and regal. Viv did her best to mimic that vibe.

They walked through the country club.

Viv realized that she didn't need this place. She had thought it was sophisticated and cool. But in reality, it was the opposite. She absolutely knew the puffy sleeves and dropped waist, southern belle dresses were so out of fashion. She knew the style those girls sported was almost over. Viv was wearing what everyone here would be wearing in a year. But probably more like two years. She knew it.

She also realized Libby was the exception here, not the rule. Nothing but total dweebs at this place.

"I hope they didn't get to you too much?" Libby said as they made their way to her car.

"No...I mean, a little. I'm proud of my outfit, but it still hurts when someone is making fun."

"Of course, it does. Those mean little trolls have no idea."

"Thanks, Libby, for coming to my rescue."

"You didn't need me to. You were doing the exact right thing. You are above them."

"Still, it's not bad having you sweep in like the Legend of Billie Jean and tell them what's what!"

"My pleasure. But that Brock, what a tool!"

"Right, he looks like John Taylor but acts like James Spader."

"Right? Hey, let's head over to Nora House. We'll pick up J.J., and Hope can get Goldie. We'll have our own dance."

"I love it."

Chapter Twenty-One

Viv Present Day

She remembered the dress, she remembered the boy's smile, she couldn't remember the faces of those nasty girls, but what stood out, more than any other image, was Libby.

And then later, the fun they'd had at her house.

Years later, she and Goldie were talking on the phone, and Goldie pointed out that Nancy Kerrigan, the skater, was wearing costumes that looked a lot like that dress Viv had designed for her ill-fated night at the club.

Ha, she'd been the Vera Wang of Irish Hills!

Her friends loved her style and trusted it before anyone else had.

Viv was warmed by the happy memory as she walked out to the deck to find her old friends, those same Sandbar Sisters, ready to enjoy a day on the raft.

"Hello! I think we picked the perfect day!" Viv was bright, her smile genuine, her joy hard to contain. She had a dark secret that soon she feared would overtake everything again. So today, she would not let it. Today, they'd be the five Sandbar Sisters.

"Oh, I swear, I did such a good job on your hairdo. I wish my hair would do that too!" J.J. said as she assessed the sassy hairstyle Viv now rocked, thanks to J.J.

It was all floppy layers in front and stacked in the back. There was shape and style now. Viv really had let it go before she came back to Irish Hills.

"I'm loving it," Hope said. And she ran a hand through Viv's do.

"I think you might have too much curl for this," J.J. said.

Hope's hair looked as strong as she did. It was iron mixed with snow mixed with the old dark chestnut.

"Don't change your hair. If I had your color, I'd be letting it fly all the time," Viv said.

Viv looked at her other friends. Goldie was still highlighting her hair, as was Libby. Goldie was California blonde, and Libby's auburn hair was her calling card.

Meanwhile, Goldie had spied Viv's bag of goodies. "Okay, what's that?"

"I made a kaftan for each of us. I refuse to worry about how I look in bathing suits or, God forbid, shorts, and from what I hear about Siena's sales, I'm not the only one."

"No kidding, every summer, Old Navy is the best place for me to get shorts and tees, and then poof, all of a sudden, I look terrible in that stuff. The shorts are too short, and the tops are, so, I don't know, what's the word? They just don't work!"

"Old Navy has nothing for us, love," Viv said.

"Right? My girls are shopping at Forever 21, and there are zero places for me," Hope weighed in.

"That's because we need high-quality fabric, we need better fit, we need three-quarter length sleeves, we aren't twenty-one, and we need our clothes to do the work."

"I need you to go with me to the store," J.J. said.

"Well, for now, here's a kaftan I made with your adorableness in mind." She handed J.J. her little gift bag and then passed out the rest.

"Ooh, is this the name? I love it!"

"Yep, Viv and Breathe, my new label." But Viv air quoted the word label. She wasn't in this for the branding or business. She was in it for joy. Maybe it would be a nice reminder to her friends, after.

Each kaftan that she'd made had a similar shape, but Viv had custom designed the length and the colors for her sweet friends. Goldie's matched her golden hair with a golden metallic shimmer. If Elizabeth Taylor could rock a kaftan in her marriage to Richard Burton, Goldie Hayes would rock one on her ponton, The Cleopatra. J.J.'s was a vibrant tangerine with turquoise trim. Hope's was cobalt blue with silver accents, it set off the silver in her hair. And Libby's was a passionate purple.

"Purple? Are we sure redheads can wear purple?"

"I'm now in charge of your wardrobe, and you can wear purple."

"Befits a queen!" Goldie said dramatically, and it was true that was what Viv had been thinking when putting together the kaftan for Libby.

Her friends admired their new kaftans. They thanked her, modeled them. Viv loved each unique piece. This would never work on department store shelves. The individual crafting of the garment was the fun of it for her.

The Sandbar Sisters gathered their stuff and walked out to the dock.

Between the dock and the pontoon and the peddle boat, Libby had everything they needed.

"Do you have some SPF 30?" Hope asked.

"Are you kidding? I have SPF 5,000. I don't spend all this

money getting my skin the texture of baby butt and then fry it out here." Goldie handed Hope a high-end bottle of sunscreen.

"I don't care what you say. My legs look good tan," J.J. said. She'd kept the kaftan on but hiked it up.

"Tan fan looks better than white fat, remember that?" Viv said. "That was our philosophy, remember?"

"Back when we weren't fat," Hope pointed out.

"If I was the size now I was when I used to think I was fat twenty years ago..." Viv said. Why could women never appreciate the way they looked, in the present moment? She knew she wasn't alone.

"Yeah, it's warped. That's where Siena and the rest of that generation have it right. We were brainwashed into thinking there was only one size," Goldie said.

"Yeah, if you weren't the shape of Cher, you were fat," Libby agreed.

"Sickening. It messed with my head for years," J.J. groaned. "Jackie subsisted on Tab Cola, Virginia Slims Menthol, red licorice and Dexatrim. Her four food groups."

In truth, all five of them were different shapes and sizes. And to Viv, they were all beautiful: curves, straight edges, sags, and wrinkles.

They laughed over old stories, commiserated over needing readers, and spent the day like they had so many times before. They'd made a pact to turn off their phones and leave them in the house. It was blissful.

By four, it was past time to go inside and call it a day. Viv didn't want it to end. But before they separated, it was Goldie who brought it out in the open.

"What gives, Viv?"

"What?"

"I know there's something more on your mind. You're sort of already gone. And I know for a fact from Siena that you're healthy."

The rest of the Sandbar Sisters dropped their various conversations, and they all floated over to the raft. They sat around Viv, and she decided to share what she knew in her heart to be true.

"I don't want Siena to know. She's worried enough. Tag doesn't know, Bret, no one."

"The fact no one but us knows that you let Randy Barton feel you up behind the grocery store is proof we can keep a secret," J.J. said. Libby punched her in the shoulder. J.J. punched her back.

Viv laughed and remembered that little moment of teen life.

"True, so very true. Okay, so it's back. The cancer is back."

None of the girls said anything, but Goldie reached over and put her hand on Viv's. The other Sandbar Sisters did the same. They all reached out in some way to each other.

"How do you know? What's happened?" Libby asked.

"I'm in pain. The back wall of my chest, it's just back. This is a bad sign, so soon after all my treatments."

"Oh, honey," Hope whispered.

"I'm going to U of M tomorrow. Tag's doctor, actually, a fantastic woman. Anyhow, she's going to see me to confirm. I just don't want Siena to go or know. She's living her dream right now, thanks to you, Libby, and I don't want to spoil it."

"She'd want to be there," Goldie said.

"I know, but I don't want her to be. This is going to go south fast. She'll have plenty of time to be there if you know what I mean."

The Sandbar Sisters listened to her, they offered love, and they offered Viv the space to say what she really thought.

"If anyone says you got this," she warned, "I'll punch them in the throat."

"*We* got that," J.J. said and put a protective hand over her throat.

"Now, let's stop talking about it. Clear?"

"Clear," her Sandbar Sisters replied in unison.

"Let's stay out a little longer," Viv suggested.

They all agreed.

There were rough waters ahead for Viv, but she didn't need to speed into them. She floated calmly with her friends on the raft, and the gentle waves kept the worst of her fears at bay.

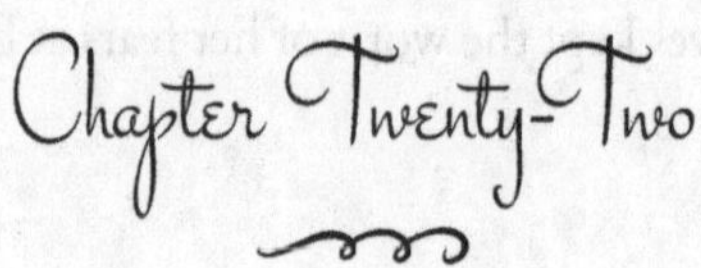

Chapter Twenty-Two

Viv

Dr. Anderson had done Viv a favor. She knew that. But still, waiting in the exam room felt like time no longer existed.

She waited, she let her mind wander, and she tried to focus on all the good things that had happened in the last few weeks.

Maybe it would be good to just go back to the lake and distract herself. Maybe just let whatever her body was doing do it. Could she stop fighting? Had she already?

She was in the middle of a new kaftan, it was an overcast day, but sometimes a rainstorm was the perfect time to sit and watch the water. Clouds moved and shifted. The threat of rain changed the air. The tall grass swayed and danced, none of which happened on a hot still day with zero clouds. She could be there, not here.

But she was here, in the very nice exam room. She had no complaints about the accommodations, but the air here was heavy. Expectation and disappointment hovered in the shadows. Other women, just like her, sat in this very spot and got the news.

She was no different than they were. They were probably

more upbeat, to be honest. Maybe she would face this next bit with less negativity. Maybe they bought into "you got this" and it worked.

She heard a little commotion outside in the hallway. Well, maybe Dr. Anderson was finally out there and headed her way. She swallowed hard; this was it.

There was the polite knock. Viv had long since dressed, and she sat on the table, fully clothed, with her sweater neatly folded on her lap.

"Come in."

And a gaggle, a literal batch of hens clucking and pecking and acting like they owned the roost, tumbled into the space.

"What in the heck?" Viv asked, but she already knew the answer.

"Yes, we used my celebrity and Libby's imperiousness to get back here," Hope said with a smile.

"You forgot my winning sense of humor," J.J. added.

"Oops, yes, that too!"

Viv tried not to cry. Why did she want to cry?

"You guys!" She dabbed the corners of her eyes. She was holding back tears because this *did* make it better.

Yes, she wanted to face this without leaning on her too-mature daughter. She wanted to be strong. She knew she could be.

But in truth, seeing her friends, old made new, helped her realize that she didn't have to do it alone. They were not going to let her get this news by herself. Even if she thought that was what she wanted.

"Wow, this place is posh," J.J. said.

"Yeah, pretty nice digs for a doctor's office," Viv answered.

The four women arranged themselves as best as they could in the exam room.

"I mean, is it just me, or do you hide your underwear in your other clothes when you go get the yearly," J.J. asked.

"Oh, I do that," Hope replied.

"You're nuts. They're about to see everything, for goodness's sake," Viv said.

"Yeah, but I do it anyway. I do not know why," J.J. said. "How about you, Libby?"

"Me?" Libby stood straighter and gave the impression this line of questioning was gauche and beneath her dignity.

J.J. and Hope looked at each other.

"I never wear underwear, so it's not an issue," Libby said.

J.J. and Goldie nearly collapsed in giggles.

"You're going to get us kicked out," Hope warned but was also trying not to lose it to hysterics.

There was another polite knock on the door. The laughter stopped, and Viv answered again.

"Come in."

Dr. Anderson walked in.

"Well, it's a GNO in here," Dr. Anderson said.

"Sorry, I suppose this breaks some sort of rule," Viv said.

"Look, we're her team. We have to be here," Goldie said.

"Oh, oh my, Goldie Hayes, I love your work."

"Thank you so much." Goldie then shot Viv a private look to say, see, told you. The doctor is a fan. There will be no cancer.

"Well, I have the results. If you want your team here to support you, that's fine, or we can go to my office."

"No, let's do it."

Viv put her hands out. J.J. took one, Goldie took another, and Hope and Libby linked with Goldie and J.J.

They were a chain. Linked together for Viv as the next few words came.

Dr. Anderson put a few x-ray films on a light board. They showed lungs and ribs but not much soft tissue to speak of on Viv's chest to get in the way.

Dr. Anderson pointed to the ribs. "You have a broken rib here." She pointed to a tiny little line, smaller than a thread. "It's hairline, as you can see, but it's there."

"Is this a result of the treatment or the next phase of my cancer?" Viv asked. She thought this was probably bone cancer or rib cancer or some new other flipping cancer.

"As you know, we biopsied several areas of soft tissue. I checked your current scans with the ones you have back in New York, and we did blood work. We took a biopsy. We did the entire work up today."

Viv knew this to be true, she'd been poked and prodded, and it really hadn't phased her.

Here's where Viv braced herself. Here's where the shoe was going to drop.

"No trace of cancer. Zip."

"But the rib?"

"This is a result of some sort of strenuous activity. It is nothing to do with cancer. In fact, you're clear as a bell in that department."

"Wait, I—the pain I'm feeling, it's all *right here*."

"Yes, and the reason is you've either lifted something or jumped into something or twisted funny. You've hurt yourself, Vivian Blackwood, but it's not cancer. It's well, I hate to say it, you're out of shape."

"Out of shape?"

"Yes, have you been partaking in strenuous activities?"

Viv thought about the last few days.

"Sewing, that's hardly strenuous."

And then Libby piped up. "You moved dozens of boxes for the store."

J.J. then chimed in. "You jumped off that stupid rope swing."

Viv felt her face get red. She was embarrassed and relieved at the same time.

"Girl, you're not relapsing. You're just old!" Hope said and squeezed her gently. "I strained my sciatica moving a jug of olive oil. It was killing me. I went like this"—Hope did a tiny twist motion—"And BAZINGA, I couldn't stand up straight or sit in a chair or anything for two months. Like *this*, and that was it."

"Oh, I have you beat," J.J. said. "I woke up, and my neck was wrenched beyond all recognition. Do you know how? I slept wrong. *Slept wrong*! I can't stand it."

"Yeah? Well, try this. I can't paint my toes anymore without getting vertigo. I lean over and get woozy. Also, can't see them, so there's that," Goldie added.

"Stop, you're making me laugh. It hurts to laugh," Viv said. But it hurt in a good way. Hurt in a way that let her know she was alive; it wasn't some harbinger of death.

"As much as I've enjoyed meeting you all," Dr. Anderson said warmly, "I have some patients waiting. I'm recommending no lifting of anything more than five pounds—no, what was it?"

"Rope swings," J.J. said.

"Yes, no rope swings. And ibuprofen, and I'm prescribing you some topical cream that will take care of the discomfort while you heal."

"No wrap or anything?"

"No, it just has to mend on its own, and it will."

Viv had tears in the corners of her eyes. She was feeling too many emotions. She couldn't pinpoint if they were good or bad.

Dr. Anderson cut through the cacophony of Sandbar Sisters once again. "You're healthy. It's gone. I consulted with your doctor in New York. We did all the tests. It's gone. It's okay."

"Thank you." Viv could barely get the words out. She wanted to say more. *I thought I was dying. I had accepted it. The dark cloud was getting bigger. And poof, it's okay. I'm okay.* But she just said thank you.

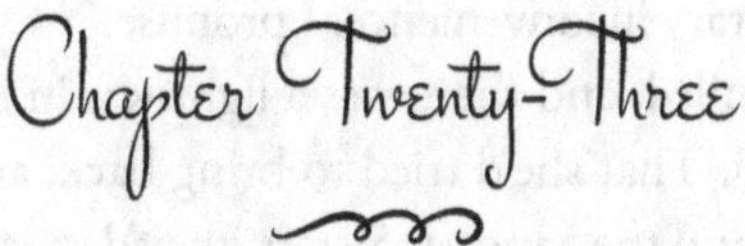

Chapter Twenty-Three

Siena

Siena was in early, as usual. The back seat of the car was packed with six new kaftans to add to her collection. Her mother had also put a label on each one.

Vivian Blackwood's new design moniker, Viv and Breathe, wasn't a design house nor a play for a big market-dominating clothing brand. It was just handmade kaftans.

Her mom said it was her mantra, not her brand.

Siena had learned, when she visited her mother's rooms at the hotel, that Vivian Blackwood had been keeping secrets from her.

"I can't carry them. It turns out I've screwed up my ribs."

"What?"

"Yeah, all this activity and no conditioning has turned me into an old lady prematurely, but Tag says he's got a trainer. We're both going to get buff."

"Why didn't you tell me you were injured? I could have taken you to the doctor! Mom?"

Siena was alarmed all of a sudden.

"Honey, you have taken me to plenty. You've got a business to grow now. You don't need to keep nursing me. Actually, no one does. I'm happy to say."

"Except you have a broken rib?"

"Psh, temporary inconvenience. I promise."

Her mom smiled, and there was a lightness in it, a sparkle that Siena had missed. That she'd tried to bring back, and maybe, with the help of Tag, and the Sandbar Sisters, they'd succeeded in doing.

"So, the elephant in the room," Siena said. "I'm staying in Irish Hills for a while at least. Are you staying?"

Siena wanted her mom to stay in this little town, but if her mom was healthy? Siena had decided she would stay no matter what her mom decided.

"Well, I can't stay at a hotel the rest of my life."

"True, but well, let's just agree that we're going to figure something out here."

"Agree, now get to work. The Siena Blackwood home décor empire isn't going to take over the world unless you're there, giving world domination orders."

"But does that mean you're staying?" Siena confirmed. "We're staying?!"

"That's what I said, now get out of here, future CEO."

Her mom thought she could be anything from a supermodel to the president of the United States. Cute but annoying. Siena was just trying to keep her store shelves stocked and figure out how to navigate her new romance with Cole.

"Mother," Siena rolled her eyes at her mom.

"Mother," Viv imitated Siena's annoyed tone. It was good. It was how it used to be. No eggshells or fake positivity in sight. Her mom seemed like her old self.

Siena got to work at the shop and unpacked the boxes of new kaftans.

The day was going to be hot. That might mean that they were slow, as most people would be out on the water.

That might be a good thing. Siena had to do some work figuring out how to style the powder room vignette she'd arranged. It currently looked like a child's bathroom and not a vacation retreat.

Maybe replace the lace-trimmed hand towels? Siena mulled it over and clicked open her laptop.

There were inquiries about hours. *Michigan Lake Live Magazine* wanted to do a story on the store. All good things.

Siena was excited to find a place here in Irish Hills. She had an idea of turning her living space into a lab, where she tested her ideas. Now that she was on this path, she wondered how it had taken her so long to realize it. It seemed so obvious.

A rattling noise outside interrupted her train of thought.

What was that?

She walked to the front window. Things were still outside.

What had made that noise? She looked up at the sky. The normal, impossible blue that had started her morning had turned yellow.

Chapter Twenty-Four

Viv

Goldie and Viv were in the kitchen. Joe, Goldie's gorgeous contractor, filled a Yeti with coffee. The kitchen was not gorgeous, Viv realized.

It was a hub of staging activity for the buffet that the Two Lakes put out for breakfast and lunch. Goldie said the kitchen was the last on her reno list since it wasn't for the guests. It was for serving the guests. Something about its summer camp vibe made Viv happy. It was the last vestige of kitsch left untouched by Goldie. Viv liked hanging in the kitchen.

"What's on your agenda again?" Goldie asked Joe, who looked at Viv.

"She asked me this last night, and then she promptly got on a phone call." He pretended to be irritated, but it was clear. He had more patience with Goldie than even her best friends did at times.

"I'm going to head out to Cedar Point Road. Tag's hiring me for his place, thanks to Viv."

Joe raised the Yeti to her in a toast.

"There's so much potential, you'll see. It's a mid-mod gem. I have so many plans," Viv said. She rubbed her hands together as though she was an evil Bond villain.

"And while I'm out there, there's a lot that Viv wants me to look at," Joe said.

"What now?" That got Goldie's full attention.

"Yeah, I've been out to Tag's a million times, as you know," Viv told her. "And there's a double lot around the curve, I'd say less than a quarter of a mile away. Anyway, the lake frontage is decent, but it's undeveloped. I want Joe to see if it's workable for a new build."

"Oh! I love, love, love it!" Goldie did a little wiggle in her chair.

"Don't jump the gun. It could be a sandy mess. I need Joe's professional eye."

"Sure, sure. But you're moving here, and that's that."

It was tough to argue with Goldie Hayes. It always had been. She had a vision, she made it happen, and she was going to insist on a happy ending for everyone in her life.

"She's pig-headed; pretty, but pig-headed," Joe said. He kissed Goldie on the top of her pretty head, and she groaned but with a smile.

They were about to go take on the day. Tag was all set to pick her up and look for a truck. Siena said she needed something huge for the business and didn't have time. So, Viv and Tag had their assignment for the day. Find a truck for Just The Thing.

She heard Tag pull in.

"Okay, well, off we go."

"Maybe you'll find a place to build the perfect house and a truck in one day," said Goldie.

"We've been taking up space in your gorgeous hotel long enough. You need rooms for the tourists."

"There's no time limit. I just figured you'd be here all summer. Blocked it out, actually."

"How in the world did you know I was going to be here more than, what, two weeks?"

"Libby said so. She did the same with me. I don't question the woman anymore. She's part city planner, part witch."

"Ha, maybe!"

"Wow, the sky looks weird," Goldie said as Viv and Tag headed to the car.

"Later," Viv said.

"It's gonna be a hot one for sure," Tag commented. He closed the convertible to make use of the air conditioning.

"I appreciate the air. So, did you decide?" She posed the question as Tag pulled the car out on to the road. She didn't want to make it a big deal, if he wasn't ready to talk about his own future. She had been in his shoes.

Tag had confessed that his hearing loss and potential for it getting worse, had forced him to reconsider his future.

"I met with the crew. I talked to the sponsors, yes."

"Well?"

"I wanted to run it by you."

"Me? You know I don't know a thing about your business. I mean, left turn, left turn, left turn."

"Yeah, yeah. But you do know about change. Big change." That much was true. Viv had decided a lot lately. She felt lighter and happier because of it.

"I'm going to retire."

He hesitated on that last word, retire.

"Because?"

"I've done a lot; I have big wins under my belt. Money in the bank. I used to think that the track was the only thing that made me really happy."

It was Viv's turn to hesitate. She wasn't ready for a big commitment or a wedding bell. She was barely ready for today.

"What are you saying?"

"I'm saying let's see where this goes. I'm going to fix up my place. I'm going to invest in drivers, instead of drive. Well, I'm going to drive you around. That's the exception."

"Because I make you?"

"No, because I like it."

"Oh, well, that's something." They were touching lightly on their feelings. That was where Viv wanted to be. "I'm relieved to hear this. Driving is a dangerous job. I want you around. I think you're making the right decision. Shifting gears on a career can be amazing, I promise."

"Plus, my hearing impairment is at the perfect level. I can hear you some of the time."

"What?"

"All of the time might be way too much."

Viv punched Tag on the shoulder. And then, to her surprise, she leaned over and kissed him on the cheek. He looked over at her and gave her what only could be described as a smolder!

Viv was not ready for smolder. She sat up straight and pretended she missed it.

Viv didn't want roses. She didn't want drama. She felt her emotions had been so raw over the last year. The easy way she felt when she was with Tag was better than big romance. Little romance was just fine.

She turned her attention to the mission of the day.

But she had a little smile that would not go away. Darn it if people started thinking she was cheerful. After all she'd done to cultivate her dark side.

They were headed to the car lot at the end of Green and Lake Manitou. If they didn't find what they were looking for in Irish Hills, it would be a little day trip to Jackson.

The weather report called for humidity. The muggy air could mean a chance of pop-up showers. She had a little umbrella in her bag, just in case.

Tag talked about what he thought Siena should have in a truck to make sure she could use it for the store. Tag was the expert in this, and Viv deferred to him. While Siena was the boss at Just The Thing, Viv was still the main investor. She knew the budget, and as long as it fit the budget, she wasn't too worried. They'd find a good vehicle. It made her happy to help Siena and not the other way around.

Tag parked at the lot. Viv gout out and a gust of cool air blew up Viv's skirt.

"It was hot and humid just before. What the heck?" It was a strange shift from just a few minutes ago at the Two Lakes.

In less than five minutes, the temperature had to have dropped thirty or more degrees. It was almost chilly.

Viv looked across downtown, and beyond, toward the lake. And the yellow sky had turned pitch black.

Sensory memory is stronger than anything else. The smell in the air. The sound of the birds, they were screaming.

Viv knew what this was. She'd been in these exact conditions.

The air was the same, the sudden shift in temperature, and worse, the inky swirl in the sky.

The conditions were identical to the tornado that hit Irish Hills in 1989 when she was a kid.

"We need to get inside, *now*." Tag saw it too. He was pulling her by the arm toward the dealership offices.

"But Siena—"

"—Viv, don't. What are you doing?" She broke free from Tag.

Vivian didn't know if Tag was following her or not. She didn't feel her cracked rib or anything else as she raced across the street to the store.

The wind swirled around the street, switching directions, and pushing her sideways.

All she could think of was getting Siena to shelter.

"Siena!" She called for her daughter as she opened the door to Just The Thing. A gust of wind pulled the door out of her hand and nearly tore it off the hinges.

"Mom, jeez, what the heck?" Siena emerged from the storeroom with a pile of linens in her hands.

"We need to get to shelter. Now."

Tag ran into the store a moment later, and then they all heard a wail.

"What is that?" Siena said.

"It's a tornado siren," Tag replied.

He went back outside as Viv looked around the store.

"We need a basement or a cellar."

"Hope's restaurant has a cellar," Siena said.

"Come on." Viv reached out for Siena's hand.

"But the inventory? I can't lose it. Maybe I grab just the—"

Viv cut her off. "No, it's just stuff. We have to go."

Tag led the way, and all three moved down the block to Hope's.

It was early in the day, and there was a distinct possibility that no one would even be in the restaurant. Viv sent up a prayer that they could get in. They didn't have time for a Plan B.

That prayer was answered when Hope opened the door to the restaurant.

"Come on, hurry!"

Siena was inside, and Tag pushed Viv to follow. But she stopped, for just a second, to look back over the trees toward the lake.

Across Lake Manitou, the dark clouds had aligned. It was no longer a mass but a distinct cone.

"There it is!" she exclaimed as the cyclone twisted across the lake. She could see debris, even this far away. As it moved you could see a cloud of debris. The debris was likely homes, trees, cars, anything in its path.

"Is that Two Lakes? Or Nora House?" Viv asked, knowing no one could answer.

"We need to get in. It will be here fast," Tag said.

"MOM!" Siena called to her.

Viv remembered the last time this happened. How a second's delay could mean making it to safety or being whooshed up into the vortex.

As if the cyclone saw into her memory, it lurched closer. It decided to head for Irish Hills instead of into the farm fields.

Viv knew it was coming for them, straight for them. She hoped all her friends were safe. She hoped that they remembered the lessons of that summer in 1989.

There was no time to do anything but dive for the cellar now. Hope, Siena, Vivian, and Tag joined Braylon Brady and Lila in the wine cellar of Hope's Table.

The walls were thick, which was good. *This cellar has been here longer than just about anything in town*, Viv thought. It had survived before. That was good.

"Come on, center wall," Tag instructed. And they all crouched close together as the wind grew to a roar.

How fast was it moving? The dark cyclone she'd witnessed was wide. If it hit downtown Irish Hills, would they survive? Even in the cellar?

"It's got to be here," Hope said. Twisters plowed through and skipped up. They were capricious. Half the horror was how one house could be totaled, another spared. Viv squeezed her eyes close.

Viv felt a pop in the air accompanied by a brief silence, and then they heard glass shattering. Was it the restaurant? Or the store?

Siena and Viv held hands. No one spoke. They were in the middle of it, the roar, the darkness. The lights blinked out. It was pitch black in the cellar.

But in an instant, the roar faded.

There was wind and maybe rain, but not the freight train sound of the cyclone above them.

Light poured in from the basement window. They were all here. They were in one piece.

Hope and Viv locked eyes. They'd been through this exact thing together.

They both knew that horror that could greet them the moment they walked out of this space.

What had the cyclone hit? What had it spared?

Chapter Twenty-Five

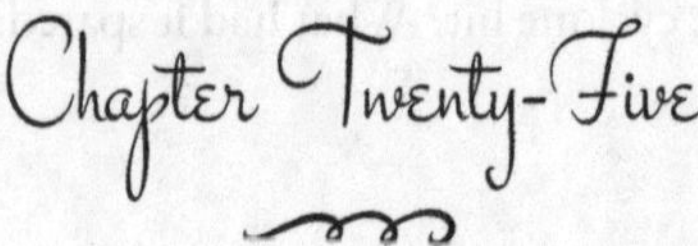

Siena

Her mother had run to her, wrangled her, and herded them to Hope's, all while a vicious storm bore down on them.

Siena looked at her mother now and saw her anew. The shell of the woman she'd become, thanks to cancer, was gone. Her mother was strong. Even with her injury, she was bold. Even in the face of terror.

She'd run across the street to Siena. She'd taken charge.

Her mother was calm. She'd actually been calm throughout, but she'd been urgent. Siena watched a look pass between her mom and Hope.

"Let's go," Viv said, taking charge again, sure that it was time to go back upstairs.

As they climbed back up the steps into the restaurant, Siena's positive feelings about this new Viv Blackwood turned to shock.

The entire front window of the restaurant had blown in, and the tables were upside down. It was as if someone had shaken the building like a snow globe.

"We need to get out of here. There could be a gas leak," Hope said as she looked over at the big stove she cooked with each night.

"That means you, too," Viv said. And she put her hand out to her friend.

They all carefully sidestepped glass as best they could and made their way out to the sidewalk.

It was hard to process what they were seeing. Downtown was a patchwork of things untouched, and others unhinged.

Siena looked toward her store.

Their side of Manitou Lake Road was littered with leaves, debris, and some glass, but it was okay.

It looked okay.

Her sign was gone, but unlike Hope's window, Siena's was intact. The buildings were all still standing.

It wasn't until the wider view of downtown came into focus that Siena truly realized the power of the tornado.

On the other side of the street, things looked much bleaker. A tree that had been in the center of the street was uprooted. It had landed on the gazebo.

But across the street, where the new work was being done, it looked horrifyingly worse.

The buildings that lined Lake Manitou on the North Side had been designed as a lovely reflection of the South Side. There were eight, side by side. It was Libby's next big project.

But right now, it was hard to process what was left.

The roof that Dean Tucker had just installed was gone, completely ripped off. Siena worried about the weather pouring into the building.

A wall on the anchor end of the block looked gone, just totally missing.

Siding on one façade had blown clean off. What once looked neglected now looked almost bombed out.

Where did Aunt Libby go from here? And was she okay? Siena

had no idea what mess the twister had caused outside of downtown.

Siena's eyes wandered down to the end of the street. She gasped. It almost made her dizzy. The landscape was so altered it made her question her own vision.

The grocery store was leveled. Not the roof, not broken glass, just leveled. There was debris everywhere, but the building had been obliterated.

"Oh my God, Barton's," Hope said. She quickly got out her phone.

"Greg." Her boyfriend Greg was the only law enforcement in town.

"Yeah, I'm okay, but there's major damage downtown. No, I'm okay, I promise. Yes, of course."

Hope ended the call and turned to them. "We're supposed to be careful. Watch out for downed lines, don't touch anything."

"But what if someone was in the store?" Siena said.

"Yeah, let's get over there and see if we can help, see anything."

They heard a different kind of siren now. The wail of the tornado siren was continuous. The scream of emergency vehicles pulsed over the top of it.

"Where's Dean?" Hope said.

Siena's memory raced to where she'd seen him last. "He was in this morning. Before all this, he was always the first one down here." Siena had gotten used to the greeting from Dean Tucker.

"HairDo or Dye," Viv said. And they all turned their focus from one end of the street to another. The salon was there, unlike the total decimation of the grocery store.

J.J. worked at HairDo or Dye. She had likely already been in for the morning. Siena tried to recreate who she had seen before she went into the store. Were people missing? As she processed, Viv, Hope, and Tag headed toward the salon.

"There, there's J.J.," Viv yelled. And J.J. emerged with the owner, Shelly. J.J. supported the older woman.

"Oh, my goodness, are you okay?" Hope asked.

J.J. nodded. Shelly looked shocked.

"The store is destroyed," she mumbled.

"No, no, it's okay," Siena said. Siena was lying. She looked back toward the salon, and it was standing. But it looked, off, as though it was lifted and set back. It was in the same place, but it was a fun house, somehow.

The sirens in the distance got closer.

Hope and Viv circled J.J. She hugged them. Siena tried to assess and orient herself. The dark sky had cleared in almost an instant.

The tornado was gone, or it was gone from their line of sight.

Was it landing somewhere else? Where had it landed before it cut through downtown?

And then the numb feeling ended. It ended with a question. It ended with the sound of Aunt J.J.'s voice.

"Dean, where's Dean?"

J.J. tried to pull away from them and head back to the wreck of the salon.

"What do you mean?" Hope and Viv held J.J.'s hands as she tried to explain. Words tumbled from her mouth.

"He pushed us to the center. He blocked the door. He was there, and then he wasn't. Where's DEAN!" There was a new wail, and it wasn't a siren.

It was the cry of J.J. Tucker as she searched for her husband.

They all began to fan out. Tag supported Shelly; Shelly cried. Where was Old Man Barton? Was he in the store when the twister hit? There were people milling about. It felt like chaos.

Deputies, E.M.S., power company vans, all of them began to trickle in.

But the question remained: Where was Dean Tucker?

Libby arrived downtown. Her house was okay, she said, but their big tree had been torn up by the roots and blocked her drive.

She'd driven her Jeep around it and pressed ahead. She said power lines were littering M-50.

Goldie called Viv and Libby. She said the hotel was okay. They had room for anyone who was displaced.

It was a constant checking in and touching base. More emergency vehicles were downtown than people, it seemed to Siena.

The weather was calm now, even pleasant. Within an hour, it was a gorgeous sunny day. But all of it seemed grotesque. A sick feeling was in Siena's stomach. J.J. had to be stopped from picking up dangerous debris with her bare hands.

Soon the sound of chainsaws slicing through limbs replaced sirens.

Everyone was trying to help, assess, and process.

The body of Ned Barton was discovered 500 yards away from his store.

He was the first casualty reported.

But the question remained. Where was Dean?

Siena pitched in. She missed a call from Cole. She called him back.

She was okay, and he was too. He wondered if she could manage on her own.

Cole and Keith were fighting to keep two boats docked at their place from sinking. They'd nearly been swamped when the wind caused a major swell at the marina.

She was fine, yes, it was okay. Shaken but okay.

But the question remained, where was Dean Tucker?

And then the question was answered with a sound worse than sirens or the roar of a tornado or a chainsaw.

"No!"

J.J. had her answer. The sound of her scream was the sound that stayed with Siena.

They found Dean Tucker.

The tornado had plucked him up and taken him away.

The body of Dean Tucker was found one hour after the tornado hit. One mile away, by a farmer.

The aunts were there, surrounding J.J., but Siena knew there wasn't one thing any of them could really do to help her.

Siena looked up to the sky.

It was impossibly blue.

Chapter Twenty-Six

Libby
Two Weeks Later

Libby sat in the office. She had set up in the vacant retail space next to Hope's Table.

The office Dean had set up for her across the street was wrecked. The tornado had blown away all the initial work Dean had done to start rehab on the south side of Manitou Lake Road.

Libby had to admit things did look better as she looked out the front window and across their little downtown.

It was a much-improved scene along Manitou Lake Road in downtown Irish Hills. Utility companies had repaired lines. Volunteers gathered debris. And broken windows had either been boarded up or replaced. That was a lot of work in the two weeks since the tornado.

It should comfort her to know that they could rebuild. This town had nearly been wiped off the map once before. This time, it fought back, fast.

In fact, Mayor Eastland continued to check with her. He

wanted assurances that she wasn't quitting. That she wasn't going to leave town like so many did in 1989. Libby had bailed then. But then again, she was a teenager. She wasn't in a position to do anything.

The mayor was in her face the day after the tornado hit. When she was still helping bail boats with Keith and picking the glass up at Hope's Table. When they were taking shifts sleeping on J.J.s couch. Before her sons got into town.

"We gave up millions from Stone Stirling. If your plans don't move forward, we're all screwed. Do you understand that?"

"I know, we're okay. We're going to be okay. This is a setback, not the end."

"You better be sure of that."

She knew Mayor Eastland wasn't the only one who had misgivings about going with Libby's renovation versus cashing out with Stone Stirling while they had a chance.

She felt an undercurrent of regret, even anger, directed straight at her. They should have gotten out while they could. Libby reassured them, she cajoled, and she worked to help raise funds for repairs for things insurance didn't cover. All the while checking in with J.J. Viv had been a godsend in that department. She was coordinating food and visits and the mass of people who wanted to be with J.J.

She barely had time to mourn with her friends. Maybe when things settled down a little.

"Things are insured. We're okay. We can rebuild," she reassured the mayor, the town council, and whoever asked. And everyone asked.

Libby looked at her policies for the buildings. It had actually been hard to get them insured. She'd tried several companies and got a lot of rejections. Eventually she'd found Granite Insurance, another godsend. They'd stepped in to offer a policy over a year ago when everyone else was either too expensive or flat-out said no.

The value of Irish Hills was on paper. It was in her plans.

But she'd managed. That was one thing she was able to tell the mayor confidently.

They could start rebuilding. And they were already.

Libby wanted to be relieved about that. But it was cold comfort.

Her best friend has lost her husband. Libby herself lost Dean, too. He was a friend. A rock.

She was also devastated for the Barton family. And while she was no friend of Clyde Brubacher, her heart went out to the people who worked for him over at the golf club. His sweet grandmother Rose was friends with her Aunt Emma and kept asking why Clyde didn't visit. It was heartbreaking.

Everyone in Irish Hills was bruised but moving forward.

Irish Hills was hit, but so was nearby Brooklyn. The steeple of St. Joe's was ripped off. They had injuries too, but no fatalities.

Irish Hills had three, thanks to what experts now categorized as an F4 tornado that formed somewhere in southeast Washtenaw County, skipped down into Lenawee, and landed on the shores of Lake Manitou before hitting Brooklyn, veering north, and dissipating south of Jackson.

It was fast and ferocious.

Irish Hills had the worst of it.

Libby's phone rang. It startled her. She'd been in her head, trying to make sense of the next steps. She was trying to manage guilt. She knew that. She lured people here. She made promises. She was responsible.

Aunt Emma.

"What's up?"

"When was the last time you slept, niece?" Her aunt said guilt was a time waster, and as she was in her nineties, she did not have time for it. Libby was trying to get to that mindset but, thus far, had failed.

"Aunt Emma, there's just too much to do. And when I close my eyes…"

"Yes, that's what happens, you see Dean, you see your friend J.J., I know."

"I'm just getting through each day."

"That's all you can do, my dear. But you must sleep. Or at least be sure to eat a sandwich today, promise me?"

"I will."

"Okay, good. My senior group is taking a van to Meijer's in Adrian. Do you need anything?"

The grocery store was gone, and Meijer, thirty minutes away, was the closest place to get groceries now. Arrow had temporarily stocked more staples at the gas station, but it still wasn't big enough to be a fully stocked grocery. The mercantile also tried to fill the gap as best as they could. They moved adorable kitchenware to the side to be sure there was free water available for volunteers and anyone who needed it.

"I'm good, have a nice trip."

"I will. I've got to go! The bus is waiting!" Emma hung up.

Her rich old aunt on a bus to the grocery store instead of with Patrick chauffeuring her around would be a sight. Except the reason for it was awful. Patrick's car had been smashed by a falling limb. Thank goodness he'd made it inside Silver Estates retirement community with Aunt Emma, hunkered down when the twister passed. But it meant her aunt was without private transport for the moment.

The grocery store was gone. The twister leveled the huge building, wiped it out in a second. The pavilion had also sustained major damage. The lists she made were grim these days. The tasks seemingly insurmountable. She was Sisyphus, pushing a boulder up a hill, only to see it roll back down.

But the lists were all things. The tasks all immaterial.

It was nothing compared to J.J.'s loss.

Libby had been fueled by adrenaline at first. The emergency of it all had been gasoline to her. They'd worked to find victims, get medical treatment, and account for everyone.

That took almost twenty-four hours.

And then there was Dean.

They buried him five days after the tornado hit. Dean was a friend to just about everyone in town. His shoulders were big, his heart bigger.

Libby was in awe of how her friend. J.J. was handling all this like a champion. She insisted on supervising Hope's food at the wake. She shouldered the grief of their sons. She accepted everyone's anguish.

She took it in and let people feel better. All the while, her own loss and trauma were in the background.

J.J. was the superhero now. Libby just hated it. Dean Tucker was one of the best people on the planet. *Why?*

There wasn't an answer.

At the funeral, J.J. stood up and recounted Dean's final seconds: "He stood at the door, wide, tall, all six-feet-four of him, and yelled that I needed to get down. I rarely listened. But this time, I did. And then he winked."

J.J. was alive because she'd listened to Dean.

"He got the last word. I still can't believe that one," she'd said. J.J. delivered the eulogy with gorgeous, glowing, purpose. Dean deserved an epic tribute, J.J. made sure that's what he got.

Libby kept seeing the dark sky. The undulating black clouds that organized and swept toward them. The twister was a monster. It bore down on Nora House. She had no time to get to anyone. She only had time to run down to her cellar.

The tornado sounded like a freight train. She remembered that from before. You just cannot believe how loud it is. The roar of it.

The drive out of her place that day was one of the scariest of her life. She wanted to be fast, to get to her friends. To make sure Aunt Emma was okay.

But what would she find?

In the end, they were lucky. Everyone kept saying that.

The National Weather Service designated it an F4 or "devasting" on the rating scale. They clocked wind speeds of over 200 miles per hour.

It claimed lives, destroyed Barton's, took the roof off of the south side of the block. It had broken the windows of Hope's Table, created damage up and down Irish Hills. It lifted roofs off buildings, collapsed others, and ripped the bark off trees.

But they were lucky it wasn't worse. Over and over. They were lucky.

Libby didn't feel lucky. All her work, all the promise of Irish Hills, and all the plans she still had to complete were nearly swept away in minutes.

"Hey, lady."

There was Viv, in the doorway, with two coffees in hand. Another pillar of strength Libby had leaned on in the last two weeks, was Viv. They were supposed to be providing safe haven for Viv's recovery. Instead, she was holding Libby up, lately. And handling whatever J.J. needed.

"Come in, come in. The folding chairs are the best I can offer, sorry." Libby indicated for Viv to sit.

"Looks good to me." Viv sat down. "I'm here to give you the news first."

Libby knew what it was, and she had no energy to fight it anymore. She'd fought to get Goldie, Hope, and Viv here.

She'd promised a vibrant place for second chances, where they could re-live some of the best times of their lives. But now, they were re-living the worst. It was a crumbling mess. She was sad, resigned.

"So, when are you leaving?"

"Well, in a week."

Libby nodded. "Not even finishing out the summer, I get it." Libby wasn't going to hold Siena to the lease. How could she? "I wouldn't be surprised if Goldie beats you."

"What are you talking about?" Viv looked perplexed by the conversation she herself had started.

"It was beautiful while it lasted, is all. I'm just so sorry I couldn't make this work. That I couldn't deliver on the promises."

"What are you talking about? You didn't summon a tornado."

"I know, but well, it was the last straw. It was the universe telling me, without a doubt, that I was leading a lost cause. I'd like to take your lead. But I'm afraid I don't have that option." Libby was crying now, she had been stoic, and now she was a puddle.

Viv rushed forward to her. "Excuse me, I just came to say I bought a double lot for Siena and me. I just paid to have storm windows installed at Just The Thing. And Joe Cassidy is currently scouting trailers for me while we work with the architect. What the devil?"

Libby looked at her friend. There was a fire in Viv's eyes. There was steel in her spine. The woman who'd showed up in June with one foot in the grave was nowhere to be found.

"You're staying? Siena is staying? Even after all this?"

"Honey, you have built something here, something that is going to outlive all of us. Irish Hills isn't a rest stop or a ghost town. It's even got movie stars and sports heroes! Heck, if you're lucky, you might even catch a glimpse of Goldie Hayes or Larson Taggert. This place is happening, and that's because of you."

Libby felt the tension in her jaw release. She hadn't realized she'd been clenching it. She'd been doing it since the moment the tornado came.

Viv was staying, and so was Siena.

"Ha, and Goldie too, none of you are bailing?"

"Nope—well, actually, there is some water in the wine cellar at Hope's, and you know Keith is still bailing over at the marina." Keith had been working not stop after the tornado swamped many of the boats docked at his place.

"Ha, funny, very funny."

"You know, I had thought I was on my last leg, and I guess I am. I guess we all are. Nobody knows what is around the corner. I may be on my last leg, but I'm not lying down. I'm going to run on it, you know?"

"I am so glad you're staying, so glad you're feeling...well, what are you feeling?"

"I'm feeling needed and supported by my friends. I'm feeling proud of what Siena's building. I'm feeling hopeful, about the future, instead of dreading it. Even with what happened to Dean, I feel like we can be there for J.J. Bottom line, I'm feeling. All of the things, good and bad. All of it right here, with my Sandbar Sisters."

Libby stood up and hugged Viv again. This was not the way she had thought this day was going to go.

As she stepped back, she quipped with a grin, "You forgot to mention you're feeling flirty with Tag. I think you might be in love."

Viv laughed. "Yeah, that too." Then she became serious again. "Libby, bad things happen. But here, we're only a pontoon boat float away from figuring it all out. Okay?"

"Okay."

They hugged again. There was a lot of hugging going on in their small town lately. Hugs had replaced handshakes. Sometimes hugs were the only thing, no words seemed adequate.

Libby wiped her tears. Viv was still recovering from cancer and her broken rib, and yet she'd walked in, picked Libby up, and set her right.

Viv left Libby to her millions of phone calls and details.

Libby was in awe of her friends and confident they could do this. They could rebuild the town again, but it was because of their strength, not her own.

She went back to her desk.

They had several festivals and special events set for the summer. They'd have to regroup for at least a few weeks. They'd lose most of July, but maybe August could still work.

Libby did what she did best. She surveyed her lists. What was next?

Even though Libby had no idea how to finance all the repairs they'd need after the tornado, Viv had reminded her that she'd figure it out.

There was insurance, but they needed more than that.

They'd need to have a grocery store before anything else. She had to find out what was next with the land Barton owned. He was gone, but were the kids going to rebuild?

That was on the list, plus calling contractors and securing the dance pavilion until they could get to repairs. She also needed someone to cut the trees out of her driveway and on and on. She could do it.

Viv had reminded her that with her Sandbar Sisters, most things were possible.

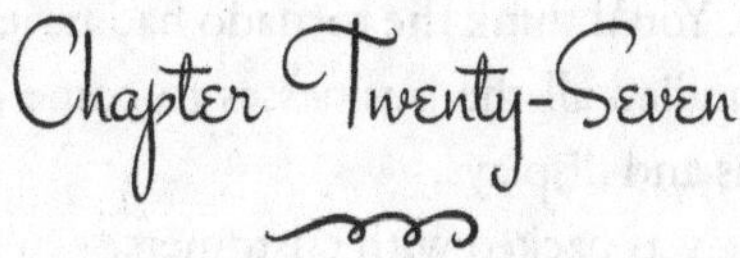

Chapter Twenty-Seven

Viv

One Month After the Twister

Summer. It was still summer. And the summer was still beautiful in Irish Hills.

Residents, vacationers, and the entire county seemed determined to remember that fact. Even though they'd been hit hard.

It was classic Irish Hills. They were going to boat, bum around downtown, ski, get sunburned, and fill the cooler with beer, tornado be damned.

And today, was a day to celebrate their resilience.

Irish Hills was throwing a party, of sorts. With Libby working on a million other things, Goldie had stepped in and taken the reigns as town cruise director and party planner.

Goldie had spearheaded a summer concert fundraiser.

She'd booked pop band Burgundy Four and country superstar River Ann for a live performance in the town square.

While insurance covered destruction and damage for some

things, the tornado had done more than what was covered. All proceeds were going to The Irish Hills Recovery Fund.

Half the town was still gorgeous and like a postcard. Aunt Emma and her seniors had worked their magic with their flowerpots and baskets. You'd think the tornado had never hit.

Goldie had rallied all the businesses to come out on the sidewalk with booths and displays.

Hope's Table was packed with customers.

The other half of the main drag was not as lucky.

One month after the tornado, the landscape of downtown still looked shockingly different.

The spot where the grocery store used to be, was now a pile of rubble. Buildings on the south side of the street were covered in tarps, and one entire wall, on what was supposed to be an anchor on that block had crumbled. Bricks continued to fall, and police barriers kept people off the sidewalk.

On one side of Irish Hills, they had adorable shops and a lure for vacationers staying on the lakes this summer. The other side looked bombed out.

HairDo or Dye had survived the initial disaster but had since been condemned. It had sustained structural damage that had to be leveled. Experts said it had quite literally been lifted and plopped down on the same spot.

Shelly, the owner, said she was too old to rebuild. She'd packed up and moved to Florida already.

Viv stood outside the main scrum of concertgoers crowding the center of downtown. Tag handed her a bottle of water as Burgundy Four played a short set for the event.

They were joined by Goldie and Joe.

"You boys see about refills? Viv and I need to head over to Siena's for a minute."

"Yep."

Viv and Goldie were on their own. They linked arms. This concert was Goldie's doing. She had stepped in while Libby took care of a million other things. Goldie was still a star, and when she called, big names answered the phone.

"I'm proud of you," Viv said as the two walked toward Siena's.

"What? Me?"

"I was just thinking that about you, getting this concert fundraiser going in the blink of an eye."

"Eh, Drake Denver is always in my debt. Trust me. You're the one who's come out of your shell, my dear. You're letting Siena fly, you're a rock for J.J. Libby told me you helped her get her head on straight. I mean, where did Wednesday Addams go?"

"She's in there, especially when I see people wearing jean shorts. I can't stomach them. I just can't!"

"There she is." A worried look crossed Goldie's face. "I had hoped J.J. would come today. It's been a month. They're even dedicating the gazebo in Dean's name."

J.J. had seemed to retreat further and further into herself. It was so different than her normal outgoing personality.

"A month isn't very long, you know that," Viv said.

"True, she put on such a brave face before."

"Yeah, she got through the big stuff, and we just have to be there for her as the little stuff tries to do her in."

They'd all visited almost every day. They'd sat with J.J. But she'd stayed home any time they tried to get her to come float on the raft or boat around the lake.

"She needs space. We just have to be on the edge when she's there, too," Viv said. They would all go to the end of the earth for J.J.

Viv was happy to see Siena's store buzzing with customers, people new to Irish Hills, and people who lived here year-round.

"Look at what our girl has got going on!" Goldie whispered to Viv.

Today, thanks to a crowd, Siena had Alison at the cash register and Cole helping take things to people's cars.

"That's looking more and more serious," Viv said.

"Wow, so maybe a wedding and babies, and we'll be grandmas!"

"Oh, boy."

"I call GiGi."

"Excuse me?"

"If Siena has a baby, I'm GiGi. You get your own name."

"I'll go by grandma. There was a minute there I didn't think I'd make it that far. Now, call me grandma, or Old Lady Viv, whatever, all day long."

Goldie squeezed her arm, and they perused Siena's latest displays.

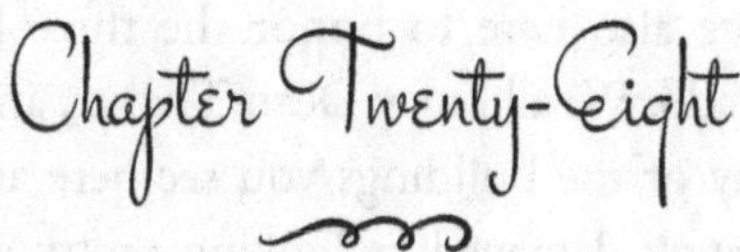

Siena

Siena and Cole closed just before sunset. They'd greeted dozens of customers on the sidewalk, helped tons more in the store. Country star, River Ann, the River Ann, walked in before her show and bought the entire set up Siena had on display for her own bedroom.

"I've got a new place over on Devils Lake I'd love to have you over, get some ideas on how to make it look pretty," River Ann had asked.

They made a date and River Ann left to get ready for her part of the concert.

But things had died down as the music pumped up. Cole helped her close and they were there at the gazebo just in time for Aunt Libby's big dedication.

Cole and Siena held hands and found their way to the cadre of aunts in attendance. Siena looked around, but still no Aunt J.J. She had been scarce, it was understandable, but it still had all the aunts fretting.

River Ann, stepped back from the microphone so Aunt Libby could step forward. She thanked River Ann and Burgundy Four for donating their time to help raise money for Irish Hills. There was a huge round of applause for that.

"Today, we're also here to honor the three lives lost to the devastating tornado. We all knew Dean Tucker, and because of his hard work, many of the buildings you see here are still standing. The gazebo, though damaged, is looking pretty good, don't you think?" Libby said.

The crowd clapped, and Libby was right. The gazebo was one of the first things to look back to normal in the days after the twister.

The idea to name it for Dean was a no-brainer. Siena watched as they revealed a brass plaque: *Dean Tucker Gazebo, in memory of a man whose strength will live on in the very foundation of Irish Hills.*

Siena teared up. Cole put an arm around her and gave her shoulders a comforting little squeeze.

Libby talked about the dedication of Clyde Brubaker to the recent improvements at the Irish Hills Golf Club and let folks know the golf club was still considering the best way to honor him going forward.

And then it was time for the Barton Family. Their business had been wiped out. Gone. But more than that, their patriarch, Ned Barton, had died. He was Alison's great uncle, Siena had learned. It was a small town, and there were several people related to Ned trying to pick up the pieces. Alison said everyone loved her Uncle Ned, though she secretly complained that he was always grumpy.

Ned's son Randy Barton had moved away years ago but was in town to handle his dad's affairs. Aunt Libby introduced Randy, and he took a moment at the microphone.

"I'm grateful to see all of you, old friends. On behalf of the entire Barton clan, I'm just thankful for all the nice things you've said. Over the years, my dad had met every single person in this county, I think."

Ned Barton had been 88 and around longer than anyone save Aunt Emma.

"As you know, the grocery store was a mainstay, a tradition, really the heart here in Irish Hills. And we know it's been a lot of people pulling together to go shop in Adrian and to help stock Arrow's. We just know it's not the same without the store."

"We loved your dad," Libby said and patted Randy on the arm.

Siena knew there was a lot more going on behind the scenes. Libby was doing all she could to help the Barton Family see the wisdom of rebuilding. Irish Hills needed a full-service grocery store, that was without question.

Siena was confident Libby would figure it out but was also glad all she had to worry about was her own store, not the entire future of Irish Hills. Libby Quinn had the weight of the world on her shoulders a lot of the time.

Libby stepped forward. It seemed like Randy was done with his remarks. But then he continued. Libby took a step back out of respect.

"So now, I want to thank someone else. He's come in, and he's going to be sure that the town has a proper grocery. I know my dad would be thrilled to know that his legacy will live on. The Barton Family would like to thank Stone Stirling and announce that he's agreed to step in and build where our store used to stand. Irish Hills will have a grocery store, bigger and better than ever, but also a true tribute to my dad."

There was a smattering of clapping, but most people just looked at one another, and a low hum of conversation rippled over the crowd.

"What are you talking about?" Libby was as surprised as anyone in the audience. She was standing close enough to the microphone that it broadcasted her shock to the entire crowd. Loud and clear.

"The family has just completed a deal with Stone Stirling! Isn't that great?"

"Randy, with all due respect, we've been trying to keep big developers out. We talked about a lot of solutions, not Stone."

Siena felt her face get hot. Aunt Libby's persona in public was usually smooth as silk. Right now, she looked like a volcano about to blow. The formal part of the event was clearly over. This was not on the program.

"Oh boy, Libby's going to be a firework finale up there," Cole said. He seemed to be inching closer. Siena stayed by his side.

But it was Aunt Goldie to the rescue. She ran up to the stage, dragging Drake Denver behind her. She stood between Aunt Libby and the mic.

Aunt Libby clearly had no clue that her shock and conversation were still the main attraction. The conversation continued. It was animated by Libby waving her hands to make some sort of point, but at least her words were no longer broadcast to the entire town. Aunt Goldie started clapping, and the crowd followed her lead.

"Great news, okay, so one more time, Burgundy Four is going to give an encore."

Siena kept her eyes on Aunt Libby, whose attention was on something that caught her eye behind the gazebo. Libby pointed and yelled. "You, are you kidding me?"

"Start, start!" Goldie said to Drake, who did what Goldie said like he was used to the role. Burgundy Four started playing the opening chords to their hit, "Summer Smile." The song was allegedly written about Goldie. The crowd forgot about Libby and her confusing outburst. They were clapping for the song. The show, behind the stage, continued.

"Come on, let's go," Siena said to Cole. "We need to see what's happening."

They wormed their way around the audience and back behind the Dean Tucker Gazebo.

They stood there and watched the much more interesting performance.

"You are kidding me, you slimy son of a—" Aunt Libby was about to say something when Aunt Hope stepped in front of her.

"Calm down," Hope said.

Randy Barton stepped in next to Stone and said angrily, "You, you rich people, are all the same. Do you think I can afford to rebuild? My dad didn't have insurance. We were screwed when that tornado hit, and along with losing my dad, we got nothing from it. Rebuild? No chance. You get it, Libby?"

"I'm sorry, Randy, but give me a chance. I could maybe get Whole Foods or Fresh Market or something to sweeten the pot for you."

"We signed a deal with Stone, it's twice what any of them would offer."

"You can't just let a fox into the hen house, Randy. Let me figure something out so that you don't need to be in bed with the big corporations."

But Randy Barton was done with negotiations. He'd gotten his money and was ready to get out.

"I'm out of here. I left this stupid place for a reason." With that, Randy Barton stormed off.

Cole whispered into Siena's ear. "It's lucky Alison's from a different branch of the Barton family tree."

"No kidding, that was not pleasant," Siena muttered.

They inched closer, and now Aunt Libby was toe to toe with billionaire Stone Stirling. Randy Barton was out of the picture. It was Stone Stirling that had Libby's full attention.

"What kind of vulture swoops in after a tornado and takes advantage of people?"

"Excuse me?" Stone put both his hands up like it was a stick-up.

"You heard me. You know we don't want you here."

"I paid the Barton family, and everyone in it, three times the value, not two. I did it because they had no insurance. I could have gotten the land for pennies."

"So now what? You're the big hero," Libby snarked.

"Does Irish Hills need a grocery store?" Stone asked coolly.

"Yes, of course."

"Well, I'll get you one."

"What's the catch?"

"The catch is you stop fighting me."

"That's not happening," Libby said. Stone put his hands down. He stepped back. He was calm and cool to Libby's fire.

"I don't want to interrupt the event. It's a nice event. We'll talk another time when you're not insane."

"Insane!"

Stone walked away, and Libby had to be restrained by Hope.

Viv and Hope circled Libby in an attempt to calm her down.

"Your aunts and your mom got this, do you think? Should I go get Stone back here so she can, uh, finish?" Cole asked. He seemed to want to go after Stone, or punch something if the need arose. Cole had a protective streak; Libby and his dad were a thing. Siena could easily see Cole adding muscle if he thought Libby wanted him to. That would not be a great idea. Siena decided to do her part to cool the overall temperature of the situation.

"If anyone does, they do. It's fine. She'll be fine."

"Wow, I thought Libby was going to murder a billionaire in the middle of a Burgundy Four concert. That would have been something."

"Yeah. Same."

Siena's mom came over to Siena and Cole.

"We're going to get Rocky Balboa over to Hope's for a calming glass of wine."

"She did not handle that well," Siena said.

"There's a lot of history," Cole pointed out.

"I probably need to find out more on that score," Siena admitted.

"Exactly, well, Cole can fill you in. See you, kids, later, okay?"

"Okay."

Aunt Hope, Aunt Libby, and Siena's mom left. Burgundy Four was now singing to Aunt Goldie. The crowd loved it, maybe they'd remember that, instead of the weird way Libby and Randy Barton left things.

Cole took her hand. His attention was fully on Siena.

"What are you in the mood for?" Cole asked.

"How about a nice quiet drive around the lake?"

"Sold. These GenXer Women are scaring me."

"Ha, same."

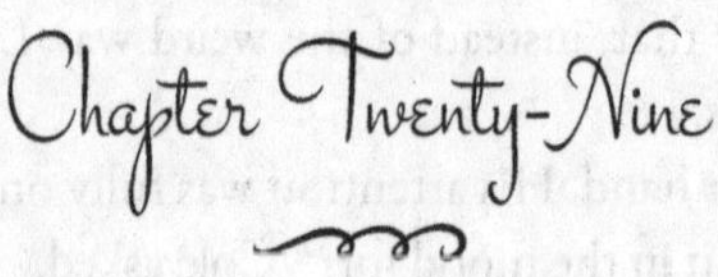

Libby

Libby sat with Viv and Hope and tried not to drink her wine too fast.

She failed.

"How in the world did I let this get by me?"

"You're too hard on yourself. The man has money, but the Bartons don't. He helped them out. It will be fine," Viv soothed.

"You weren't here for the worst of it. He tried to bulldoze Irish Hills out of existence."

Hope backed her up and nodded to Viv, who looked wide-eyed at the thought of it. The work she'd done to stop it was all upside down now. Nature and a billion dollars had conspired to undo all she'd accomplished.

Also, she'd lost her cool in front of, uh, everyone.

"It was bad," Hope said to Viv. Then she turned to Libby, and added, "But he didn't get anywhere, though. You won."

"Yeah, but this is sneaky, this is some way to horn in, and I don't know what, but it's not good," Libby said. She put her head in her hands. She didn't have a list for this.

Goldie showed up a few minutes later.

"Hope, you good if the band and all 'em come here? Their set is almost done, their surprise set," Goldie remarked and looked pointedly in Libby's direction. A fresh wave of embarrassment washed over her.

"Yeah, you got her?" Hope was referring to Libby like a hand grenade with the pin pulled. "I need to get back to the kitchen to help with the rush."

"Viv and I will handle it," Goldie said.

"I'm right here, you know. I can hear you." Libby was trying to calm herself. She was trying to think like Stone Stirling.

"Man, you really flipped your lid," Goldie told her. She poured herself a glass of wine from the bottle.

"Yeah, yeah, I did."

"I think J.J. and Dean would have liked that. Memorial-wise, it was a lot less boring with your eyes bugging out and yelling at a billionaire. Really livened things up. You don't normally see threats of violence at charity fundraisers." Goldie was laughing now, and so was Viv.

"Ugh, okay, okay," Libby said, "it was totally out of line. I get it."

"Over here," Viv called out to a group entering the restaurant. She waived Joe, Tag, Greg, and Keith to their table.

"Wow, I thought I might have had to put the cuffs on you, slugger," Greg said to Libby.

"I didn't throw a punch. I wanted to, but I didn't."

"It'll be okay." Keith kissed her on the cheek.

"Did you see?"

"No, I just got here. I had to close up the marina."

"Well, I'm sure it wasn't as bad as they say," Libby said. But she knew it had been a scene. She was calming down, though. The wine was helping. And having her friends here. They were more amused than scandalized. That was something, she guessed. "Did I overreact?"

"No, you just reacted normally, but in front of the entire town...and a mic," Goldie said.

"Oh, man, I'd have paid to see you punch that guy in the face," Joe said.

"I don't know. He seems alright to me," Tag said.

Libby shot daggers out of her eyes at him.

"Ouch, I felt those," Tag groaned.

Hope popped in and out as they all settled in at their corner table.

Libby wanted to get to her phone and her lists and to plan her strategy now that Stone Stirling had a foothold in Irish Hills. It was exactly what he had always wanted. How had she not seen it coming?

But Keith held her hand. Hope served up some Nosh Plates. Goldie regaled them about the money Burgundy Four had raised for the Irish Hills Fund. And Viv just radiated something. Happiness. She was happy. Viv had the best perspective of all of them.

Libby calmed all the way down.

She realized that she had these people to help her, to go to battle with her if need be, but mostly to have a glass of wine with when the going got weird.

She feared she had a new fight ahead. But maybe she didn't.

No matter what came next, she'd made the best decision in her life by reconnecting with her Sandbar Sisters. Thanks to Aunt Emma.

She raised a silent toast to her aunt.

And then she looked around.

She wished J.J. was here. That was the missing piece. J.J. and Dean.

Libby had lost her cool tonight. She needed to be patient. She needed to trust that this would work out.

And she needed to let J.J. heal in her own time.

She lifted her glass again. This time, the toast wasn't silent.

"Hey, let's drink to Dean. I miss him so much, and I just know he'd have been there telling me not to murder Stone."

"Or helping you bury the body if you did," Keith added.

They all raised their glasses.

"To Dean!"

She'd live to fight Stone another day, and Dean would be there in spirit.

She just hoped J.J. would be there in person.

Chapter Thirty

J.J.

J.J. could hear the sounds of Burgundy Four through the windows of the house. She knew she should be there for the dedication, but she couldn't do it.

The well-wishing was suffocating. Everyone was lovely. But she was having a harder and harder time breathing lately.

She didn't want to see anyone. She was tired of being the brave face. This was the perfect time to do what she'd planned.

"Are you sure?" her mom asked. J.J. went through a little mental inventory. Did she have everything?

Jackie Pawlak was worried, and it was sweet. Although, she'd expressed her worry by smoking twice the number of cigarettes than normal. Dean would have laughed at that, J.J. realized. Ugh. She couldn't tell him that joke. Was that ever going to end? She kept wanting to tell Dean something funny, or weird, or annoying.

"Hey, listen to this," she'd say.

Dean would say, "All ears."

"And beard," she'd say back.

It was corny, they said it every time.

If she hustled, only her mom would know what she was up to.

"Look, Mom, you can have the place the rest of the summer. Jared's going to be by every day to make your high balls. It's all good." Jared thought she was going away for a few days, which was fine. He'd figure it all out.

"But your friends are here. This is your home."

J.J. looked at her mother, who'd been more motherly the last month than she'd been for J.J. and Jared's entire childhood. "Mom, this is really Dean's home. It was. I need to be somewhere that every square of carpet or swatch of paint isn't something he did. You get it?"

"I get it, baby girl."

Jackie was sitting at the slider, cigarette out the door, but the smoke wafted in anyway.

"And just because I'm going does not mean you can smoke in the bedroom or the living room, got it?"

"You're so bossy. I got it."

"I'm all packed. I'm going to get moving."

"It's kind of sneaky that you're doing this while your friends are all at the gazebo thing."

J.J. agreed. It was sneaky. But she didn't want them to talk her out of it. "I know. It's just for a little bit."

"You take what you need, don't worry about the old house. It'll be here when you get back."

"Not if you burn it down with these things." J.J. took the cigarette out of her mom's hand and snuffed it out in the empty Coke can her mom was using as an ashtray.

"Ugh, boss, boss, boss." Her mom hugged her. She smelled of White Rain hairspray and Virginia Slims. It wasn't an unpleasant smell. Actually, it was just Jackie.

"I'll text you when I get there."

"Sure, okay. And the boys, they know?"

"Yep, my kids are all living their lives. They don't need to worry about me dropping my basket for a bit."

"You remember when I dropped my basket after that dirtbag hit me?"

"Yeah, a little bit," J.J. lied. She remembered everything, but what good would it do to make her mom feel bad about that water under the bridge?

Jacqueline Pawlak was a heart breaker in her youth. But she'd been on the other end of it too, too many times to count. Her wacky mom was a survivor.

"Okay, okay. I love you, sugar."

"Love you too, Jackie." J.J. kissed her on the cheek.

That's where I'll leave her. It's peak Jackie, with that cig, thought J.J.

Her mom was sitting in the kitchen Dean had remodeled, at the table he'd fixed when it was wobbly. J.J. walked out the screen door he'd patched when the boys put a baseball bat through it.

She could go on and on. The light he installed over the porch. The driveway he sealed. It was endless. And it was overwhelming. The memories of their life together were lovely, mostly. They'd had their share of trouble, especially those first fifteen years.

She remembered picking him up, at the lockup. Oh, boy did they fight after that.

Her life was in that house. Her messy wonderful life. But things had taken a turn for the tragic. She needed out.

J.J. got in the car. Dean had the oil changed just a few weeks ago.

"What do you think the red light means?" He'd asked her when he'd seen it on.

"It means, tell Dean, when you think of it." She was notorious for ignoring her check oil light. Dean handled it.

She would need to skirt downtown and the celebrations that were underway. It was sweet, dedicating the gazebo. She knew her friends wanted her there. Dean probably would too.

J.J. pulled out of the driveway.

Her mind went back.

She thought about the first time she laid eyes on the big lug of a man, Dean Tucker.

They were both so young. J.J.'s Sandbar Sisters were all off, having lives. She was still here. A townie.

She was done with high school but had no real idea what came next. There was no college money. No trust fund. She was doing nails and shampooing clients for Shelly back then, at the HairDo or Dye.

J.J. remembered her state of mind. It was restless the night she met Dean.

She'd taken her fake I.D. to Michigan Tavern, it was hopping on that Friday night. All her local high school friends were there. It was nice. But she was bored. Nothing was as fun without her Sandbar Sisters.

She was at the bar, waiting for a beer, when some dude she never met started hitting on her. She told him off. Loudly. The dude didn't like it. And he got a little more menacing by grabbing her arm.

And that's when Dean Tucker, seated quietly on the other side of the dude, entered the picture. He stood up. He towered over J.J. and her rude would be suiter.

"The little lady said she wasn't interested."

"Little lady? What are we in Deadwood?" J.J. said to Dean. That was the first thing she said to him, come to think of it.

"Do you or do you not want this douche bag to continue to hit on you?" Dean looked her in the eye.

He was six-four, barrel chested, his shirt was too tight, and his pants were too loose. But Dean Tucker had nice eyes. Kind eyes. And J.J. made a choice, right then.

"I do not want him to continue to hit on me. But I don't mind if you do."

J.J. pulled onto the highway as she thought of that night, so long ago. It made her chest feel tight. Her eyes welled up at the memory. She wasn't ready to look back on the good times. Or the bad times.

J.J. Tucker was tuckered out. There was nothing left in her tank for one more sad look, one more hug of sympathy.

She wanted out of Irish Hills. She wanted out of the turn her life had taken.

J.J. didn't look back at Irish Hills. Looking back right now gave her nothing but tears.

She needed to keep her eyes clear and her hands on the steering wheel. As she drove, she did her best not to think too much. She hated her thoughts, on repeat, of how much she missed Dean.

She was mad too. Why did that dufus run to the hair salon? Or why couldn't he have been two seconds quicker and jumped inside?

Why did he have to be the hero?

Why? Why? Why?

Why was he taken away just when things were getting so good?

She'd need to speed up.

Her flight left in three hours, out of Metro Detroit.

It was a one-way ticket.

J.J.'s Story Continues in Sandbar Sunrise

About the Author

Rebecca Regnier is an award-winning newspaper columnist and former television news anchor. She lives in Michigan with her family and handsome dog. Follow her on one of her socials. She loves to share laughs with her readers!

- tiktok.com/@rebeccaregnierbooks
- facebook.com/rlregnier
- instagram.com/rebeccaregnier
- bookbub.com/authors/rebecca-regnier